HONORS FOR APRIL HENRY

Edgar Award Finalist

Anthony Award Winner

ALA Best Books for Young Adults

ALA Quick Picks for Young Adults

Barnes & Noble Top Teen Pick

Winner of the Maryland Black-Eyed Susan Book Award

Missouri Truman Readers Award Selection

TLA Tayshas Selection

New York Charlotte Award Winner

Oregon Spirit Award Winner

One Book for Nebraska Teens

Golden Sower Honor Book

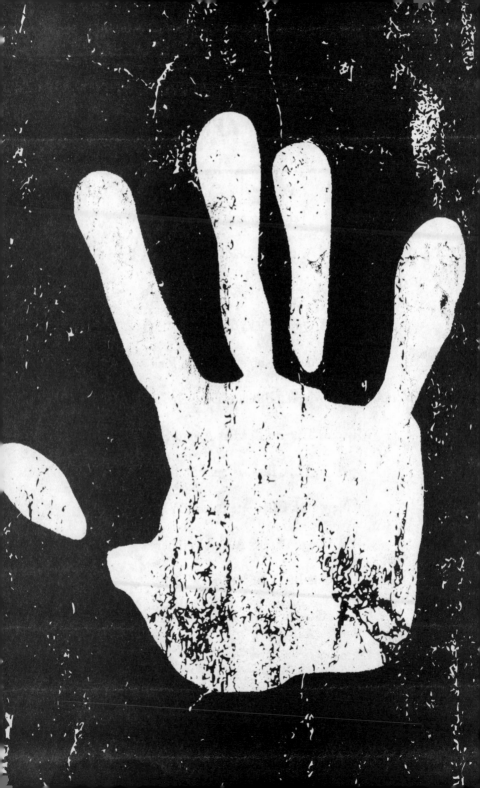

THE GIRL IN THE WHITE VAN

OTHER MYSTERIES BY APRIL HENRY

Girl, Stolen

The Night She Disappeared

The Girl Who Was Supposed to Die

The Girl I Used to Be

Count All Her Bones

The Lonely Dead

Run, Hide, Fight Back

Playing with Fire

Eyes of the Forest

THE POINT LAST SEEN SERIES

The Body in the Woods

Blood Will Tell

THE GIRL IN THE WHITE VAN

APRIL HENRY

SQUARE
FISH

Christy Ottaviano Books

HENRY HOLT AND COMPANY
NEW YORK

SQUARE
FISH

An imprint of Macmillan Publishing Group, LLC
120 Broadway, New York, NY 10271
fiercereads.com

Square Fish and the Square Fish logo are trademarks of Macmillan and are used
by Henry Holt and Company under license from Macmillan.

Our books may be purchased in bulk for promotional, educational, or business
use. Please contact your local bookseller or the Macmillan Corporate and
Premium Sales Department at (800) 221-7945 ext. 5442 or by email at
MacmillanSpecialMarkets@macmillan.com.

The Library of Congress has cataloged the hardcover edition as follows:
Library of Congress Cataloging-in-Publication Data
Names: Henry, April, author.
Title: The girl in the white van / April Henry.
Description: First edition. | New York : Henry Holt Books for Young
    Readers, 2020. | Audience: Ages 12–18. | Audience: Grades 10–12. |
    Summary: Told in multiple voices, sixteen-year-old Savannah Taylor is
    abducted after her kung fu class and must figure out how to escape and
    rescue fellow prisoner Jenny Dowd.
Identifiers: LCCN 2019037073 | ISBN 9781250157591 (hardcover)
Subjects: CYAC: Kidnapping—Fiction. | Kung fu—Fiction. | Mystery and
    detective stories.
Classification: LCC PZ7.H39356 Gih 2020 | DDC [Fic]—dc23
LC record available at https://lccn.loc.gov/2019037073

Originally published in the United States by Christy Ottaviano Books/Henry Holt
and Company
First Square Fish edition, 2021
Tire tracks @ pingebat/shutterstock
Book designed by Mallory Grigg and Angela Jun
Square Fish logo designed by Filomena Tuosto

ISBN 9781250791993 (paperback)

10 9 8 7 6 5 4 3 2 1

AR: 4.9 / LEXILE: HL690L

To Bruce Lee

Notice that the stiffest tree is most easily cracked,
while the bamboo or willow survive by bending
with the wind.

—BRUCE LEE

SAVANNAH TAYLOR

WITH A GRUNT, I BROUGHT THE BACK OF MY RIGHT FIST DOWN
on the bridge of my attacker's nose. A split second later, my
left hand clawed down the face, scratching the eyes, goug-
ing the nose and cheeks.

Right, left, right, left. Each shot set up my next. Right:
leopard's paw to the throat. Left: straight punch to the
bridge of the nose. Right: roundhouse to the temple.

And then my bedroom door swung open, taking with
it the mirror—and my own reflection, which I'd been pretending was my attacker.

As soon as the door started moving, my face heated
up. Worse yet, it wasn't my mom on the other side. That
already would have been super embarrassing. It was Tim,
my mom's boyfriend.

He hadn't even knocked.

"Hey, Karate Kid! Sweep the leg!" With a smirk, he sliced his hands through the air, accompanied by cartoon sound effects. "Choo! Choo!" He was wearing a brown Carhartt jacket over dark blue coveralls. One of his work boots kicked an imaginary target in midair.

Dropping my hands, I turned away. A second ago, I'd felt so fierce. Now I just felt like an idiot.

I was mad at myself for being caught by Tim. The fact that I was still in my pajamas made me feel even more stupid. My face got hot, which meant that my pale skin was betraying my feelings.

Saying nothing, I picked my library book about Bruce Lee off the floor next to my bed and slid it into my backpack. I'd checked it out in the hope it would teach me some cool kung fu techniques, but it was mostly about philosophy.

Reminding Tim that I was taking kung fu, not karate, would just prolong things. It was actually his face I'd been imagining while attacking my own reflection. He was my least favorite of all the guys my mom had ever lived with.

Tim finally stopped making sound effects and karate chops. "Do you really think any of those moves would work in real life?" He took a step closer. "You're just fooling yourself taking those stupid classes. If some dude really wanted to hurt you, you'd be toast."

Don't respond, don't respond, I reminded myself as I grabbed a sweater and jeans from my closet.

He switched gears. "Your mom's taking me to work today. So make sure you lock up when you leave the house."

Tim's "classic" Camaro had broken down. Again. It was

kind of ironic, given that he was a mechanic. Normally my mom was still asleep when I left for school. She worked swing shift as a CNA at a nursing home.

"Okay," I said, still not meeting his eyes.

After making a sound that was halfway between a snort and a grumble, Tim finally left. I heard the bathroom door close. There went my chance of a shower.

The first thing I did was lock my door, the way I should have earlier. As I got dressed, I fumed. Bruce Lee said that to survive you had to bend, I reminded myself as I pushed my feet into my black-and-white-checked Vans.

In the kitchen, my mom was loading the dishwasher. Tim always left his dishes wherever he finished eating— the dining room table, the arm of the couch, even the bathroom counter. He must have dealt with his own dishes before we moved in, but now it seemed to be "women's work."

"Good morning," Mom said with no conviction. Maybe she was finally starting to sour on Tim.

"You must be tired." I poured myself a bowl of Life cereal and sat down on one of the two black kitchen stools.

"I can take a nap later if I need to." As she put a mixing bowl in the back of the dishwasher, her sleeve rode up her arm.

I pointed at a spot on her wrist between tattoos. "Mom, what's that?"

She hastily pulled down her sleeve. "Nothing."

"That's not nothing. Those look like bruises." Four round dark dots in a row, each the size of a fingerprint. Someone had grabbed her wrist, and it wasn't too hard to guess who it was. Even though I sometimes had the same marks, at least mine were from escaping practice wrist grabs in kung fu. Not from the real thing.

She forced a smile. "He didn't mean to. And he said he was sorry."

"You can't let him treat—" I stopped midsentence as Tim walked into the room.

"What are you girls talking about?" He looked from my mom to me and back again.

"Nothing," Mom said. At the same time, I said, "What to make for dinner tonight."

"None of that vegetarian crap. I need real protein. Something with meat." Tim's grin was flat. "Come on, Lorraine, let's go."

After they left, my stomach was churning too much to let me finish my cereal. My mom refused to see how bad things were. And even when her eyes were finally opened, she would just do what she always did when things went sour: meet some new guy online and then jump out of the frying pan and into the fire. Using a profile photo that was nearly as old as me, Mom had met and fallen in "love" with men all over the United States and then moved in with them sight unseen. Before Tim in Portland, Oregon, we had lived with Garrett in Houston, Texas; Adam in Hebron, Nebraska; Brandon in Brookings, South Dakota; and Paul in Saint Charles, Missouri. And before them were five or six other guys and places I'd already forgotten about.

Pretty soon there would be another move to be with another man who would invariably turn out to have lied about himself and his life, in ways both big and small.

Before we moved here, Tim told her that he owned the auto body shop he only worked at. The house was half the size he'd said it was. I was pretty sure he had even claimed a few extra inches of height in their conversations.

He and my mom had managed to make it work for seven months. That was practically a record. But their arguments were getting more frequent. Which meant it was probably time for a change.

The thing was, I liked Portland. You could be yourself here, and people appreciated that. Portlanders took pride in the Unipiper, a guy who wore a Darth Vader mask and rode a unicycle while playing the bagpipes. Vegans, Wiccans, transgender people, recumbent bike riders, stand up paddle boarders, people walking their pet goats, guys with elaborate beards, girls who didn't shave their legs or pits, guys wearing utility kilts, people with rainbow hair, tattooed hipsters with huge gauges stretching out their earlobes—people who would have been mocked in many of the towns I'd lived in—were celebrated here.

And despite Portland's reputation, it didn't even rain that much.

As I locked the door and set out for school, I did the math again. In one year and seven months, I would be eighteen. Old enough, in the eyes of the law, to live on my own.

SIR

MY HANDS WERE SLICK ON THE STEERING WHEEL. MY FOOT hovered over the accelerator of the old blue Chrysler New Yorker, my chosen vehicle for the day. I was going less than five miles an hour, but I didn't touch the pedal. Outside it was close to freezing. I left the defrost button alone, even though I could barely see out the windows. The fogged glass provided cover. I had rubbed a small section of the windshield clear, enough to see straight ahead.

Just enough to focus on the girl about a block ahead of me. She had straight brown hair and wore jeans and a bright blue puffer coat. She glanced over her shoulder. When she saw the car, her eyes narrowed. Turning back, she started walking faster, nearly scurrying.

My own heart sped up. Humans are built to hunt. Like any predator, when they see the prey start to run, they want to give chase.

Only was she really the one? I couldn't afford to make another mistake. Instead of pressing my foot on the accelerator, I pulled over and took my notebook from my pocket. The car was quiet except for the sound of my breathing.

Dec. 7. 7:50 a.m. Corner 36th & Kamin. Tall. Straight dark hair. Bright blue coat. Alone.

I underlined *alone* twice. But where did she fall on the one-to-ten scale? I thought about her dark hair. Then considered her face, with its slightly receding chin. Finally I added a number.

7.

But after thinking about the long legs under her jeans, I added a dash and a second number.

7–8.

And then I began to hunt again. Hunt for the perfect girl.

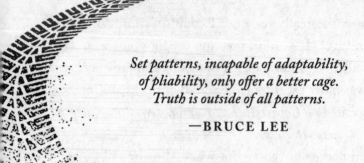

Set patterns, incapable of adaptability,
of pliability, only offer a better cage.
Truth is outside of all patterns.

—BRUCE LEE

SAVANNAH TAYLOR

WITH A BATTERED METAL FORK, I PULLED A LONG GRAY-GREEN
strand of something that had once been spinach from the
school cafeteria lasagna and let it drop onto the brown plastic tray. Somehow the spinach managed to be both stringy
and gaggingly soft.

I was sitting by myself. Three or four schools ago, I'd
decided there was no point in making friends if you were
only going to move away again. You could promise you were
going to still text or Snapchat, insist you'd keep in touch on
Instagram, but it was never the same. Pretty soon people
who used to be your friends were as distant online as they
were in real life.

I was pretending to read my Bruce Lee book, but really
eavesdropping on the conversation at the next table.

"It's just so scary!" Alice's voice slid on the last word.
She sounded delighted.

"What is?" Latoya asked as she set down her tray.

"Courtney said some dude in an old blue car was following her this morning." Preston popped a baby carrot into his mouth.

I shivered. For the past couple of months, rumors had bounced around school about a driver trailing girls on their way to or from school. The car was never the same, though. One time it had been a black Oldsmobile, dented and boxy. Another day it had been a beat-up brown pickup with an aluminum cover over the bed. But no matter what kind of vehicle, they all had three things in common. The windows were always fogged up. The vehicles were always old and dirty, down to mud-smeared license plates. And, according to the stories, the driver was always careful to hang back about a block, drifting forward about the same speed as the girls walked.

Latoya shrugged. "It was probably just somebody looking for a house number. Pure coincidence. You know Courtney. She's always convinced that it's about her."

"But there was that girl in Beaverton who disappeared from Island Tan, like, a year ago," Preston said. Beaverton was the next town over.

"I heard that she just ran off with the bank deposit," Latoya said. "That that was missing too."

"Then why'd she leave her car behind?" Alice asked. Her gaze suddenly sharpened. I realized she was looking straight at me. Crud. My face got hot. She had caught me staring. Even though I immediately looked away, it was pretty obvious that I'd been eavesdropping. Time to leave. Careful not to look in her direction, I got to my feet and then picked up my book and tray.

As I was scraping the remains of my sad lasagna into

the gray rubber garbage can dedicated to compostable food scraps—very Portland—someone behind me said my name.

"Hey, Savannah."

I turned. It was Daniel Diaz. We knew each other from kung fu. In class, it was hard to keep my eyes off him. I told myself it was because he had such perfect form. He could do a spinning hook kick that made him look like a human helicopter. He was a senior, so we didn't have any classes at Wilson together. But almost all the other kung fu students were adults, which gave us a kind of bond. At least I was always hoping it did.

"Oh, hi." I felt my face flush again, but for a different reason.

In kung fu, I was just an orange belt, one up from white. Daniel was a green belt, only two ranks below black. He had been taking kung fu for five years. Some martial arts schools routinely promoted students every few months, without really making them prove themselves. But our school prided itself on not being a belt factory. There were adults in our classes who had been going for longer than Daniel but who weren't much higher in rank than me.

"So you're reading about Mo Si Ting?" Daniel asked as he scraped his plate into the bin.

"What?"

With his fork, he pointed at my library book. "That was Bruce Lee's nickname when he was a kid. It means Never Sit Still."

"Oh, yeah." Did my responses sound as stilted to him as they did to me? "Everyone always says he was the best. I was hoping I could pick up some new techniques."

10

Daniel tilted his head, making his thick black hair fall over one eye. "And have you?"

"So far, it's mostly been a lot of sayings," I admitted, setting my tray on the rubber motorized belt.

Daniel set his tray next to mine. "That might make sense, actually. Bruce Lee wasn't a big believer in memorized techniques. He thought martial arts had become too stylized, so that they weren't practical anymore and wouldn't work in a real fight. For him, any technique was good as long as it was flexible and fast, without a single wasted motion. He called it 'the style of no style.'"

This was the longest conversation I had ever had with Daniel. "The style of no style," I repeated, secretly blessing the Multnomah County Library. "I like that."

People were stacking up behind us. I saw a few of them noticing Daniel noticing me. By unspoken agreement, we moved into an empty corner.

"Which of Bruce Lee's movies is your favorite?" Daniel asked. "Mine is *Enter the Dragon*. That scene where the bad guy escapes into the hall of mirrors and Lee has to deal with all those reflections of himself. It's epic!"

"I actually haven't seen any of them all the way through," I admitted. "Just the bits and pieces you can watch for free on YouTube." I simultaneously winced and smiled. "Like that one scene where he's fighting Chuck Norris and he yanks out his chest hair and then blows it off his hand." I mimed Bruce Lee's actions as I spoke.

"*Way of the Dragon*," Daniel said immediately. "Which is good, but not as good as *Enter the Dragon* or *Fist of Fury*." He grinned. "If that scene had been in *Fist of Fury*, I guess they could have called it *Fist of Furry*."

"Ouch!" I groaned at his pun.

"I've seen every Bruce Lee movie ever made. When I first saw *Way of the Dragon*, I thought maybe that body hair was fake, because when Chuck Norris turned around there were even big clumps on his shoulder blades. But when I googled it, it said it was real. It must have been cooler to be hairy in the seventies."

The bell rang, and everyone started making for the doors.

"See you at class tonight?" Daniel asked.

Nodding, I tried to respond with a modest smile. But despite my best efforts, it stretched into a grin.

> *Do not pray for an easy life. Pray for the strength to endure a difficult one.*
>
> —BRUCE LEE

SAVANNAH TAYLOR

THE REST OF SCHOOL PASSED IN A HAPPY BLUR. THERE WAS something about Daniel that left me wanting to break my rule about not making friends.

When I got home, I made cornbread and, mindful of Tim's complaint, chili with more meat than beans. The salad, I knew, would just be for my mom and me. Even as my hands washed and chopped and stirred, my thoughts were consumed with thoughts of Daniel. His brown eyes with flecks of gold. His long-fingered hands. How he was just the perfect height, so that if for some reason we ever hugged, I would be able to tuck my head under his chin.

Like always, I ate before Tim got home. Then I put a lid on the chili and left the cornbread in the oven so it would still be warm for him.

I sprawled on my bed and did homework. I tried to stay

in my room as much as possible, especially when my mom was at work and it was only Tim and me. When I finally heard the front door open, it was a half hour later than normal. He must have had to hitch a ride from one of the other guys at the shop. Tonight he didn't even try to talk to me, which was a relief. Out in the kitchen, I could hear him muttering to himself, but not the actual words. Then the TV went on.

I checked my phone. Almost time to go to class. Once it started getting dark earlier, my mom had wanted Tim to drive me, but we both insisted that wasn't necessary. And now of course he couldn't. I changed into my green T-shirt and black athletic pants, then put my book and my orange belt in my backpack. It was really more of a sash, black cotton fabric with an orange stripe sewn around one end. Passing the test for it a month ago had been one of the proudest days of my life.

That evening, a couple of other students at my dojo had also tested for orange. All of us were required to demonstrate our skills before three black belts. I only knew one of them, my teacher, Sifu Terry. But that night he was just as expressionless as the other two men closely watching us.

Off the mats, the room was filled with friends, family, and higher-ranked students. Since my mom was at work, I was alone in the crowd. The room started to feel like it was too small, like all the oxygen was used up. Claustrophobia was kicking in. With every passing minute, I felt more and more anxious. It was all I could do not to run outside.

By the time the test started, my mouth was dry, my hands damp. I vowed to be perfect but instead made mistakes. So many mistakes. In one of the forms, I punched with my left hand instead of my right. I lost my balance doing a roundhouse kick and had to set my foot down. When we were asked to demonstrate a low block, out of the corner of my eye I saw that the other students were holding their arms in a different position. Each mistake left me more flushed and faltering than the last. By the end of the test, I was blinking back tears.

It had been a shock to still be awarded the rank, to go through the ceremony of kneeling between two rows of flickering tea lights in an otherwise darkened room, and then fumblingly tie the belt after Sifu handed it to me as everyone applauded.

Now I zipped up my backpack. Class started in twenty minutes, and it took about twelve minutes to walk to the dojo. With luck, before class Daniel and I would talk some more about Bruce Lee.

As I walked into the living room, Tim was slumped on the couch, watching football, still wearing his mechanic's coveralls. At his feet were several empty beer bottles, his kicked-off work boots, an ashtray filled with butts, and a dirty bowl and plate.

He looked very little like the pictures of the man my mom had showed me. The blue eyes she had exclaimed over all but disappeared when he narrowed them. In the pictures, his shaved head had made him look tough, but now I knew that if he skipped running a razor over it for a day or two, it was clear he was just going bald.

Not sounding like he particularly cared, he mumbled, "Where're you going?"

Even if Tim couldn't remember my schedule, my T-shirt emblazoned with the school's logo was a pretty big clue. "The same place I go three nights a week." I pulled on my coat, then leaned down to get my backpack and hat. When I straightened up, Tim was right in front of me. I hadn't even heard him get up. I sucked in a breath and took a half step back.

"Are you disrespecting me?" he said through gritted teeth.

I lifted my empty hands in a placating gesture. "I'm just going to kung fu class."

"Class!" He made a raspberry sound. "That class is giving you unrealistic expectations. In the real world, you're a little girl with a big mouth." He grinned without humor. "And anyone could do anything they want to you. That class is just putting ideas in your head."

A pit opened in my stomach. Kung fu was the one good thing in my life right now.

"But I'm paying for it with my babysitting money." My inflection rose at the end like it was a question.

His face changed, and I knew I'd made a mistake. "And now you're definitely talking back. You're grounded."

"Grounded?" My voice broke in disbelief. It would have been funny if it wasn't so stupid. I didn't do any of the bad things I heard other kids at my school talking about. I didn't get drunk or use drugs or shoplift or sneak out at night.

Tim snorted, and I had the image of a cartoon bull pawing the ground, ready to charge. "Yes. Grounded. You live under my roof." He stabbed a finger at me. "You eat my food, you sleep on sheets that I paid for. But you act like you can do whatever you want. You're nothing but a spoiled brat that doesn't know how to be grateful for what she has. So I guess I'm going to have to teach you. Grounded means you go to school and you come straight home. And you don't go anyplace else."

I locked my teeth around the words I wanted to spit at him. My mom would see how stupid this was. I pulled my phone from my pocket and started a text.

Tim snatched my phone from my hand. "Grounded means you don't have a phone."

Surprising even myself, I ran for the door.

When you feel pain, you know that you are still alive.

—BRUCE LEE

SAVANNAH TAYLOR

AS TIM REACHED FOR ME, I YANKED OPEN THE FRONT DOOR and ran out. When his fingers grazed my shoulder, I twisted away in midair. Fear gave my feet wings.

I pounded down the porch steps, with him only a few steps behind. He cursed when his bare feet met the sharp gravel of the driveway. I kept running even after I heard him limp to a stop. He was still yelling threats and swears.

It was another block before I burst into tears. My pace finally slowed to a walk. What had I done? I should have just pretended to accept Tim's stupid rule for one night and then gotten my mom to sweet-talk him out of it. But now that I had openly defied him, he would dig in his heels. Sure, I'd make it to kung fu tonight, but it could easily be my last class.

And even if my mom managed to persuade Tim to

let me go again, it wouldn't fix things for long. Soon she would start looking again for the Prince Charming she was always sure was out there just waiting for her. And then we would move to some other town. When everything I cared about was here.

My breath came in hitching gasps, hanging in a white cloud in front of my face. I had to compose myself before I got to class. The cold air scoured my lungs, but my face still felt red and hot. I dried my eyes on the puffy sleeve of my coat.

With each block, the neighborhood had been changing. The houses were now interspersed with small businesses closed up for the night. I passed a day care, then a row of town houses. The warm yellow light streaming from their windows somehow made me feel even more alone.

What would happen when I returned from class? If the front door was locked, I had no way to get in. And what about when my mom got home? Would she demand that I apologize? What would I do if that happened? Or would she take my side and then they'd get in a big fight? Would Tim kick her out, too? Sleeping in my mom's car might actually be better than spending one more night in his house. It wasn't home. It was just a place I kept my things.

I could talk to a school guidance counselor. But what could they really do? Tim had never laid a hand on me. They would just say he was strict. It seemed unlikely that they would force him to give my phone back or to un-ground me.

No, the best I could hope for was my mom deciding to move on. No more kung fu. No more Daniel. I sucked in another breath and ordered myself not to start crying again.

Crossing the quiet street, I cut through a small strip mall's empty parking lot, past a dentist, a nail salon, a tax preparer, and a shoe repairer. This neighborhood was so hilly that my kung fu school was tucked underneath these businesses, on the bottom half of the building, yet all of them, including my kung fu school, had outside entrances.

As I went down the concrete steps that connected the two levels, I was so wrapped up in my own thoughts that I barely registered the old man walking up the other side of the street. Or the young man pulling his bike up at the bottom of the stairs. Or the middle-aged guy slowly driving a white van past us.

"Savannah! Hey, Savannah."

My focus finally shifted to the outside world.

Daniel. He was the guy on the bike. My face got warm again.

"Oh, hey. Sorry!"

"Didn't you hear me calling you?" He threw one long leg over his bike seat.

"I guess I was in my own world."

He looked at me more closely. "Are you okay?"

Were my eyes still shiny with tears? "It's just cold out, that's all." If I said anything about Tim, I would start crying again.

He nodded, without looking completely convinced. After locking his bike, he held the door open for me. Inside it was warm and filled with the familiar smells of sweat and disinfectant. There was the usual crowd of adults, some chatting, others stretching or practicing forms.

Together, Daniel and I took off our coats, toed off our shoes, shoved our stuff in cubbies, and then tied on our belts.

Sifu Terry called out, "Okay, let's line up." His long black hair was gathered back into a ponytail low on his head. The way he moved made me think of a jaguar.

Before I stepped on the red mat, I made my right hand into a fist and then covered it with the palm of my left hand. The right hand symbolized a weapon, and the left showed that it was controlled, demonstrating respect for the dojo and my partners.

I took my spot, second from the left. Around me, the other eight people lined up in order of rank. As the senior student, Daniel was on the far right. Until two weeks ago, I had been on the other end of the line. Now to my left was a guy with a shaved head who was always talking about how he had taken tae kwan do back when he was in high school, which had to be at least twenty years ago. It was clear he didn't think he really belonged in last place.

With a padded striker, Sifu rang the heavy metal bell. The deep soft clang hung in the air as he saluted us with the same hand-over-fist gesture, which we returned.

Right after we moved to Portland, I'd been walking by the school and stopped to watch a class through the floor-to-ceiling window. The students had looked so fierce and strong, displaying coordination I couldn't even imagine possessing. It was summer, and I was at loose ends, not knowing anyone. I started observing class on a regular basis, as if the window was really a giant TV. Then one day, when the students were practicing a new move, Sifu

Terry came out. Before I could hurry away, embarrassed at being caught, he introduced himself and invited me to try class free for a week. That had been enough to hook me. I paid for it with weekend babysitting jobs.

Now Sifu said, "Today we're going to be working on grab counters." The word *counter* always sounded weird, like kitchen counters or people who kept track of numbers, but it meant a countermove, a way to negate whatever your attacker was doing. "Daniel?" As the senior student, Daniel got the privilege—and sometimes the pain—of being the demonstration model.

Sifu reviewed the basic counters for wrist grabs. "Rather than meeting force with force, find the weak spot or use his momentum to your advantage." He showed us how to turn our wrist so that the narrowest point pushed against the attacker's thumb, the weakest part of the grip.

"The next counter is for when someone grabs your shoulder from the front." He nodded at Daniel, who grabbed Sifu's shoulder with his left hand and threateningly raised his right fist. "You swim your arm up and in, breaking his grip," Sifu said as he demonstrated with a movement like a swimmer's front crawl, "and step back to take yourself out of range." He turned toward us. "Okay, everyone get a partner and practice those grabs with about three to five follow-up moves."

I looked to my left, to Mr. Tae Kwan Do, but suddenly Daniel was in front of me. Usually students at his level stuck together, at least for the first few rounds.

"Talk to your partner about how real you want to make it," Sifu said. "If you make any contact, especially to the face, it should be kiss-touch."

Kiss-touch meant contact as light as a feather. It both demonstrated control and that you were capable of delivering a much more powerful strike.

The words *kiss-touch* applied to me and Daniel made me blush. It was all I'd been thinking about since we had talked at lunch. But that was stupid. Wanting to be kissed and touched was what had made my mom drag me over nine states in eight years.

"You grab me first," Daniel said. "And make it as real as you can."

"Same goes for me." I clamped my fingers hard around his wrist. He twisted and eventually broke my grip. A flicker in his expression made me think that it was more difficult than he expected. I smiled to myself as he threw a few follow-up kicks and strikes that just brushed me.

Then it was Daniel's turn to grab me. I was hyperaware of his cool fingers circling my skin.

Playing bad guy, he grunted, "You're coming with me." He yanked me forward.

His words reminded me of Tim. I jerked my wrist away, not even minding how it hurt, then grazed his ribs with a roundhouse kick, followed by a backfist to the nose that I turned into a gentle tap.

Class would be over in fifty minutes. And then what would happen?

Daniel and I traded grabs back and forth, until Sifu told us to switch partners.

My next few partners handled me much more gingerly. Their reluctance to hold on tightly made me angry. How was I ever supposed to learn what worked or what didn't? At the same time, I had trouble focusing, sometimes forgetting that it was my turn, while my partner waited more or less patiently.

As class went on, Sifu showed us street fighting techniques: how to twist an ear, shove a palm under the chin, dig two fingers into the notch of the collarbone. Even though Sifu demonstrated the moves lightly, it was clear from Daniel's expression that they hurt.

When we split into pairs to practice, Daniel chose me again. He did each move only until it started to cause pain and then rubbed his fingers over the spot he had just hurt, as if rubbing the pain away.

At the end of class, Sifu said, "Because we don't want to break our partners, we're constrained in what we can practice at full force. But remember, if you're fighting for your life, there aren't any rules. When you're attacked, 'fighting dirty'"—he made air quotes—"is exactly what you should do. Bite, pull hair, knee their groin, scratch their eyes." His usually playful black eyes were serious. "When your life is on the line, you have to do everything you can."

DANIEL DIAZ

WITH THE REST OF THE STUDENTS, I RETURNED SIFU'S BOW AT the end of class. But I didn't really see him. Instead, the left-hand corner of my vision was focused on Savannah Taylor. Before today, when I'd seen her with the Bruce Lee book, I hadn't paid a lot of attention to her.

I mean, sure, I knew who Savannah was. But white belts tended to come and go, try class for a week or a month and then decide they were really cut out for Pilates or pickup basketball. Even people who made it to orange, as she had a month ago, sometimes dropped out right after the test, as if they had used up all their energy just climbing the first rung of the ladder. It wasn't unusual for it to take a decade to get a black belt. If you ever did. Some people had tested numerous times for it and never been awarded the rank.

Sifu dismissed class. At our dojo, the students were

expected to clean up afterward. When I saw Savannah take one of the mops, I made sure to grab the other. Since mopping the floor was the last step, by the time we started, all the other students had left, calling goodbyes.

Sifu picked up his backpack. "Hey, Daniel, do you mind locking up tonight for me?"

"No, Sifu."

"Thanks. I promised my daughter I'd help with her homework." He gave us a wave. "See you guys Saturday."

After the door closed behind him, I was hyperaware that we were now completely alone, with the darkness pressed up against the windows.

"Tonight was fun," I said, moving the mop in a series of tight S-curves down my half of the floor. *Fun?* Couldn't I think of something better to say than that? Just the memory of Savannah's skin under my fingertips left me tongue-tied. I had dated a few girls before, but nobody special. Nobody who had made me feel the way I was starting to think I might feel about Savannah.

"Yeah." Sniffing, she swiped at her nose with the back of her hand.

Remembering how wet her eyes had looked when we met outside, I realized I'd been too focused on myself. "Are you really okay, Savannah?"

After a long pause, she said, "Right before class, I was kind of arguing with my mom's boyfriend." As she spoke, she kept her gaze on the floor.

"So he lives with you?"

"We live with him. He's the reason we moved here. But I don't get what my mom sees in him. I'm not even sure *she* does anymore." Savannah shook her head. "Anyway, we really weren't seeing eye to eye."

My hands tightened on the mop handle. "What were you arguing about?"

She sighed. "Tim says it's dumb that I'm taking kung fu. He's always talking about how it wouldn't do me any good, because men are bigger and stronger." After dipping her mop back into the water, she squeezed it dry. "But now I feel like I *could* do something if someone attacked me. Maybe I'd still end up hurt or killed, but I'd definitely make them sorry first."

"The struggle is real," I said. "Size does make a difference. But most bad guys don't have any training, and you're starting to. And you've got good instincts, and you move well." I didn't add that this Tim dude seemed like a real jerk. The kind of guy who wouldn't be happy until he brought everyone down to his level.

"Thanks." She lifted the mop head from the water and dropped it into the wringer. "I've never really done any kind of sports before."

Grabbing the handle, I squeezed it dry for her, standing close enough that my shoulder brushed hers. "And what he said about size is just wrong. Look at Bruce Lee. He wasn't much bigger than you. He was, like, five foot eight and a hundred forty pounds, and he was the best martial artist in the world. Ever. I think he would have approved of what we were doing tonight. It was certainly practical. He wanted to be able to end fights while expending as little energy as possible. And he never telegraphed what he was doing." I tilted my head. "Do you know what that means?"

Savannah gave me a crooked smile, and my stomach did a complete 360. "It's funny that we still use the word *telegraph* when none of us has actually seen one. But telegraphing"—she moved the mop handle to her left hand so she could demonstrate with her right—"that's like when you pull your fist way back for a big roundhouse, right?"

"Yup. Your standard bar fight punch. Bruce Lee's kicks and punches were more like they exploded from his body, with no windup. He was famous for his one-inch punch. People literally didn't know what hit them."

"At least you and I understand where *that* phrase came from." Savannah's blue eyes flashed up to mine and then back to the floor.

"And he was more than just a martial artist. He did fencing and running and weight lifting and boxing. Anything he thought would make him better at kung fu." I might have been a little obsessed with Bruce Lee, but Savannah honestly seemed interested. "He was even the Hong Kong Cha-Cha Champion."

She brushed back her dark curtain of hair. "Cha-Cha? Like the dance?"

Bruce Lee had supposedly only learned to dance as a way to impress girls who didn't appreciate the fact that he could do two-fingered push-ups and jump eight feet into the air. I decided not to share this with her. "I read that he realized a lot of what he learned dancing could also be useful for kicking ass."

"Well, dancing's supposed to make you light on your feet." She wasn't looking at me, but at the dirty mop water.

I clenched the mop handle so hard it hurt my fingers.

Before I could think better of it, I said, "Winter formal's next month. Wanna see if it would work the other way around? If kung fu could make us good dancers?"

She opened her mouth, but no words came out. With every second, I died a little.

Finally she sighed. "Sorry. I don't think it would be a good idea." She didn't elaborate, but I filled in the blanks. She didn't like me. She only liked me because I could throw a spinning hook kick. She had a boyfriend. She thought my obsession with Bruce Lee was weird.

Whatever it was, she clearly wasn't interested in me.

"Okay," I said, then added, "Sorry."

"No, I'm the one who should be sorry." Her mouth turned down at the corners. "I mean, I like you, Daniel, but—"

I held my hand up to interrupt her. "That's okay. You don't have to explain anything." I just wanted this moment to be over. I didn't need to hear the details. Or worse yet, a lie.

We finished the mopping in awkward silence, while I mentally kicked myself for ruining what might have been the beginnings of a friendship. For making what had clearly been a bad day for Savannah even worse. After putting the bucket and mops away, we grabbed our stuff. I set the door so that it would lock behind us, and then we walked outside. After the warmth of the dojo, the chilly air was a shock.

It was also dark, the area around our school deserted. "This part of town is so empty at night," I said. "I could walk you home if you wanted."

Her lips twisted. "Oh no, I'm okay. My mom's waiting in the upper lot for me." She pulled on her hat, then offered me a sad smile as I started to unlock my bike. "But I'll see you in class."

If you want to learn to swim, you have to throw yourself in the water.

—BRUCE LEE

SAVANNAH TAYLOR

MY FEET TRUDGED UP THE CONCRETE STAIRS I'D COME DOWN ninety minutes earlier. They were the same stairs, it was the same cold night, but I actually felt worse than I had before.

I felt even more alone. It was clear that Daniel liked me. And I liked him. I really did. His warm brown eyes made my knees go weak, as did the way his black hair fell over his eyes and the way his long fingers pushed it back.

I hadn't said no because I was grounded. I figured that would be long over by the time of the dance. But if I had said yes to going with Daniel, I knew where it would lead. To me having my heart ripped out when we left Portland, as we inevitably would. To me becoming like my mom. Always desperate to fill the missing piece.

I reminded myself that I didn't need a guy. I didn't

need friends. I didn't need anyone. As soon as I was old enough, I was going to live on my own. I was going to be completely independent. Make my own money, my own choices, my own life.

And no matter where I was, that life would include kung fu. As soon as I walked into Tim's house, I would apologize to him. If I had to, I would grovel. I wouldn't even ask for my phone back. I'd promise to cook him steaks every night. Maybe offer to polish every inch of his stupid Camaro by hand after it was fixed. Whatever it took to keep coming back to class.

At the top of the steps, I rounded the corner of the building. I was so lost in thought that I only knew something was wrong when a rough hand grabbed my wrist from behind.

My first confused thought was that it was Daniel, seeing how well I remembered tonight's lessons. Playing a joke on me.

But as I was jerked backward, I smelled cigarettes and motor oil. And I saw what I hadn't registered at first: an old white van parked in the darkest corner of the lot. The lot that earlier had been empty.

I froze, all of tonight's lessons fleeing from my head. What would Sifu do? Or Bruce Lee?

And then I remembered that rather than trying to pull away from my attacker, I should instead accelerate his motion by pushing toward him. Toward the thumb that was the weakest part of his grip. I let him spin me around and yank me back as I stepped closer. I felt my hat go sliding off as I circled my right arm up and back, breaking his grip. With a muffled grunt, he let go. My momentum carried me closer to him. I was already striking out with the heel of my left hand. His teeth clacked as I made contact with his jaw.

I turned and ran. As I did, I sucked in my breath to let out a scream. I was in a dark, deserted parking lot outside a dark, deserted building. The nearest people were at least a block away. Tucked inside their houses, warm and safe, the windows shut, the curtains closed. Still, I had to try.

But what came out of my mouth was a screech. Not a scream, not a piercing cry, not an alarm that split the night. It was both soft and high-pitched. It didn't seem to go anyplace except maybe right above our heads, hanging with the fog of our breath.

A second later, I felt two tiny stings, one in my butt and one on my right thigh. My body went rigid as every muscle clenched. My head jerked up and back of its own volition. As I toppled over, my vision filled with white light. I felt the pain in my teeth, my eyeballs, my fingertips.

And then my head hit the ground, and I didn't feel anything at all.

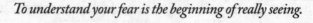

To understand your fear is the beginning of really seeing.

—BRUCE LEE

SAVANNAH TAYLOR

WITH A GROAN, I TRIED TO OPEN MY EYES. I FELT MY EYEbrows rise and my lids faintly flutter, but they were so heavy it was all I could do to finally crack them open. It didn't make much difference. Wherever I was, it was nearly as dark as it was behind my eyelids.

I also had the worst headache of my life. Each heartbeat made the pain expand and contract.

What was happening?

When I tried to raise my head, it felt as heavy as a bowling ball. And just as empty. I let it fall back.

Time passed. All I was capable of was existing. But slowly my consciousness began to reassert itself.

Where was I? I took inventory. I was sprawled in an awkward twist, not quite facedown. Whatever I was on was cold and unyielding, vibrating faintly. My breathing seemed too shallow, fast and panting.

Something was clearly wrong. But I couldn't fill in the blank of what it was.

I started to push myself up. But my wrists were bound together. I slumped back down. Slowly, I considered the possibilities. Not handcuffs. Not rope. Something wide that pulled at the hairs on my wrists.

Duct tape.

Memories slowly came back. Going up the stairs, my thoughts preoccupied with Daniel. The old white van squatting in the corner of the parking lot. The rough hand grabbing me from behind.

And I had done nothing to stop it, except for my pathetic attempt to scream. I had kept on second-guessing myself right up to the point where I had stiffened and fallen. Had he injected me with drugs? I remembered feeling stings.

Now here I was. In the back of that white van. Underneath me the metal floor was vibrating from the hum of the motor. The man who had hit me had to be driving it.

He must have gathered me up and then dropped me inside his van. I tried to remember his voice. Had I heard it before? Had it belonged to someone I knew? He had smelled like motor oil and cigarettes.

He had smelled like Tim.

But Tim didn't currently have a car, let alone a van. So the man must be a stranger.

That seemed even more frightening. If he was anonymous to me, that meant I was to him as well. Anonymous meant disposable.

But the familiar way he smelled. Could Tim have borrowed one of the dozen or so cars that were always at the shop, waiting for repair?

And whether it was Tim or a stranger, what should I do now?

Don't move, a voice whispered inside me. *Make yourself still and small. Maybe that way you won't get hurt any worse. The longer he doesn't notice you're awake, the longer he doesn't think about you, the better.*

But that was a lie my fear was telling me.

The only reason this man was taking me someplace was that the new location would be better for him.

Better for him, but not for me. And with every passing second, we were rushing farther away from where anyone would think to look for me.

So I had to cut this trip short before the van stopped and whatever he had planned for me started.

The van wasn't varying in speed, wasn't stopping and accelerating, like it would for lights and stop signs on city streets. Were we on the freeway? It didn't feel like we were going that fast, but I couldn't be sure. How long had I been unconscious? How far away were we from the dojo? Did anyone even know I was missing?

I could not keep lying here on the way to my doom.

My body felt disconnected from my brain. It was like my thoughts were taking place in a different world than the one in which I lay.

I scanned the space through the crack between my upper and lower lids, looking for anything that might help me. Slowly, I figured out that I was facing the back door of the windowless van. When I realized my attacker couldn't see my eyes, I opened them wider. My feet were closest to the back of the van, my head farthest away.

And in the middle of the rear of the van, a line of silver about six inches long.

A handle!

If I could get to it and open it, then I could escape. We were on a road. A road meant other people. People driving on the road. People living in houses next to it.

People who could save me. Even if they didn't want to get involved, they would probably still call 9-1-1 if they saw a duct-taped girl escaping from a white van.

But I hadn't heard any other cars pass. Maybe the rumble of the van's engine masked them. Or maybe by now we were way out in the country.

Even if there was no one around to help me, I could still run away. I could hide. All I had to do was get out.

But how? If I got to my knees, once I opened the door, I would just fall out face-first. I needed to keep my legs in front of me. Maybe I could even manage to land on my feet. I imagined the shock of landing, how I would take giant, staggering steps, somehow staying balanced. How I would run away in the dark before my attacker even knew I was gone.

Daniel and some of the other high-ranking belts could do standing rolls. They tucked their heads and somersaulted in midair, and when they landed on the mat, they rolled diagonally from one shoulder across the back to the opposite hip. Their heads never even touched the ground. I had always been too scared to try it from standing, but had done a modified version from my knees.

Whatever move I tried, I needed to be as close to the door as possible. Even if my captor was watching in the rearview mirror, he couldn't keep his eyes on me all the time. Plus the back of the van was nearly pitch-black. The only reason I could see was that my eyes had adjusted. He was watching a road lit by his headlights.

Holding my breath, I moved my feet a few inches closer to the door. Nothing happened. He didn't shout or step on the brakes. I scooted my butt closer to my heels. I counted to sixty and then repeated the process, worming myself a few inches closer to the handle. But I couldn't afford to be too slow. What if he was almost where he was going?

I sucked in a deep breath. Here I went. I pulled my arm under my side. I got up on my elbow and then pushed myself off the edges of my bound hands. I reached for the handle.

And missed. I fell back onto my shoulder, biting my lip to keep from screaming in pain and frustration.

Again. I had to be quick. Arm, elbow, hands, reach.

A shout behind me spurred me on. The fingers of my right hand curled around the handle.

It refused to move.

Despair flooded me even as I tried the other direction.

Suddenly the handle twisted and the door flew open into empty space. The cold night rushed in. Now I could smell how close the air was in the van, how it stank of fear. Maybe even of death. That thought spurred me on.

I leapt into the dark.

A fight is not won by one punch or kick.
Either learn to endure or hire a bodyguard.

—BRUCE LEE

SAVANNAH TAYLOR

TIME SLOWED DOWN. IT SEEMED AS IF I HUNG SUSPENDED IN midair for long seconds. There was plenty of time to think about how I might be able to land on my feet. Or launch myself into a forward roll.

Plenty of time to observe that I was actually not doing anything.

And finally I came down to earth.

My bound left wrist hit the ground first, taking most of the impact. It became a pivot point around which the rest of my body rotated. The pressure on my left forearm increased and increased, until finally I felt something in it snap, just above my wrist.

Momentum wasn't done with me yet. My arms might have come to a stop when they met the road, but the rest of me was still moving. My feet flew over my head. Somehow

I managed to keep my head from hitting the pavement. It was nothing like the forward roll I had imagined pulling off. Instead, I was slammed flat onto my back, driving all the air from my lungs.

Lying on the roadway, I looked up at the distant stars. It felt like the universe had hit the pause button. It felt like I might never breathe again. I was pretty sure I was badly damaged, maybe beyond repair. But I didn't care. I felt curiously detached.

And then my lungs spasmed. I took a jagged, involuntary gasp, and the air rushed back in.

With it came the pain. It started at my broken wrist, spread to my ribs and head, and then suddenly it was everywhere. The pain was as big as the sun, and it swallowed me.

I was broken. I couldn't fly, I couldn't roll, I couldn't walk. I couldn't even imagine moving.

I heard the van screech to a stop, and the engine shut off, followed by footsteps.

Standing over me, the man blocked out the nearly full moon. He swore. When he bent down to gather me up, I passed out.

JENNY DOWD

REX'S BARKING WOKE ME. IT WASN'T JUST A FEW WOOFS, BUT a ferocious volley.

At the sound, my stomach crammed into the back of my throat. I remembered what had happened the last time Rex sounded like that. In the dark, I scrambled backward on the bed until my back was against the wall. My hands flew up to cover my face. Under my palms I could feel the tender ridges and seams that now crisscrossed my cheeks, nose, and lips. My heart was beating so hard it felt like it might come out of my chest.

Outside, Sir was yelling, *"Sitz! Bleib!"* Finally, Rex switched to frustrated whines.

Trying to calm my racing heart, I sucked in a breath. Rex was outside. Out there, he couldn't hurt me again.

Outside there was a rattle as Sir undid the padlock.

A short length of chain had been bolted on either side of the door, and when he padlocked the ends together, they stopped the door from opening more than a couple of inches. I waited for his footsteps to shake the trailer as he made his way down the hall. Instead, he called for me.

"Jenny, get out here. I need your help."

I scurried out. In the living area, he was standing half in and half out of the door. I stopped in my tracks. Cradled in his arms was a girl. I hadn't seen another human being besides Sir for months.

Her dark brown hair hung down over his arm. Her eyes were closed, and her mouth was slack. Ripped duct tape dangled from her right wrist. There was a scrape on the left side of her face, a raw red patch beaded with blood.

"What happened? Did Rex bite her? Is she dead?" I was too shaken to think about avoiding words with *B*s. He hated how they sounded when they came out of my mouth. I kept my right hand over my face, hiding the worst of my scars. Sir had made it clear that he did not want to look at them. At me. And he had taught me to never look him in the eye. Collecting myself, I added, "Sir."

"Stupid thing jumped out of the van while it was moving. Now she's hurt. I need you to help me splint her wrist." He took a step inside the trailer. A pack was looped over one shoulder. "Close the door behind me."

I didn't move.

Sir swore. "Rex won't bite you when I'm here. Now close the door before I get really angry."

I forced myself to move, keeping both my arms up in front of me, ready to protect my throat, my face, my belly.

Rex's front paws were on the bottom step, and his ears were back. His wet white teeth gleamed as he gargled a growl. My heart leaping in my chest, I yanked the door closed with a shaking hand. When I turned around, Sir had disappeared with the girl into my room. I followed. He had turned on the light. He laid her on her back across the end of my bed. The girl didn't move. He was taking off her torn teal blue puffer coat. Underneath, she was wearing black exercise pants and a short-sleeved green T-shirt with some kind of design on it.

The left sleeve of her coat was shredded, revealing puffs of white polyester filling. Gingerly, Sir pulled down the sleeve, turning it inside out in the process. As he eased her left arm free, the girl's upper lip drew up and her eyebrows pulled together. But she still didn't wake up.

Even I could tell her left wrist was broken. Three inches above her thumb was a bump, like someone had stuck an egg underneath her skin. "I need to get the bones lined up so I can splint it." Sir began to rummage through my stuff. "And it will be better for everyone if she's still unconscious when that happens."

From the nightstand, he took one of my three magazines, the October 2007 issue of *Real Simple*. Curling it in his hands, he gave it an experimental twist. Even though I had read every word on every page, my heart still sank when he set it on the bed next to the girl.

Then he dug through the clothes in the drawer underneath the nightstand and plucked out my blue turtleneck. The turtleneck I had been wearing the day he took me. One of my last links to the time before. When he pulled the knife from the sheath on his belt, I bit my lip so I wouldn't protest.

He slid the knife inside the body of the turtleneck. Stretching the cloth tight with his other hand, he pulled until it dimpled and then split. Then he yanked the silver shine of the blade toward him, slicing the fabric. He moved the knife a few inches over and repeated the process. And again. And again. The turtleneck was being turned into strips. Finally he cut them all free.

"Now hold her arm tight just below the elbow. And don't let go even if she wakes up."

There was not enough room for both of us to be at the end of the bed, so I crawled around and behind the girl, trying not to jostle her. I looked down at her face. Aside from the scrape, her skin looked smooth and soft. Unmarked. It must be why he had taken her.

Sir rolled her on her side so that my knees pressed against her back. At a nod from him, I wrapped my fingers around the middle of her arm.

Taking her hand in both of his, he positioned himself so that her arm and body formed a line. Then he pulled.

It was like she had been shocked by a downed power line. Her body stiffened and then immediately went slack again.

He ran his fingers over the broken part of her arm. Most of the pronounced bump was gone, but it was still puffy. "I can't cast it until the swelling goes down, and that's going to take a few days."

He wrapped the magazine around her forearm, then had me hold it in place while he tied it off with strips of my turtleneck. Then he turned one of my cardigans into a sling, knotting the sleeves behind the girl's neck. The whole time, she didn't stir.

Finally, he was finished. "Pull back the covers." Picking her up, he squeezed between the bed and the wall and laid her down. After he straightened up, we both looked at her. Even in the dim light, her color looked bad to me, the smooth skin of her face pale and sweaty.

"Is she going to be okay?"

"She took a pretty hard hit to the head. I wouldn't be surprised if she has a concussion. Just let her sleep."

Careful not to raise my gaze to his face, I risked a question. "Isn't that bad, Sir? I thought you were supposed to keep someone awake if they had a concussion." Would I get in trouble for talking back? But I most definitely did not want to wake up next to a dead girl.

He sighed. "They used to think that, but it depends on the type of concussion—it's complicated. Sleep is good. It will allow her brain to recover."

"Yes, Sir."

He moved to the doorway. "When she does wake up, it's going to be your job to teach her how to act. Your job to teach her the rules." I was still silently digesting this when he demanded, "And what are the rules?" His hand moved to the butt of his Taser, as if to remind me how I had learned them.

Quickly, before he could get mad, I blurted out, "Always call you Sir." To be safe, I quickly added, "Sir."

"Don't mumble," he said. "Go on."

"Never look you in the eye." Out of the corner of my

own eye, I saw him nod. "Never talk back," I continued. "Dress attractively. Keep things picked up. Don't make noise."

"And?" he prompted.

"Be grateful that you keep me—I mean us—alive. Sir."

He nodded again. "That's right," he said. "Good girl. It's better that she learns them from you rather than the hard way, don't you think?" As a reminder, he tapped the butt of the Taser again before dropping his hand.

And then he left me alone with the girl. A girl like the one I had once been, ten months ago.

MICHAEL DIAZ

"MS. TAYLOR?" I ASKED THE PLUMP THIRTY-ISH WOMAN SHIFT-
ing from foot to foot in the school office. When she nodded, I stuck out my hand.

Despite her strong grip, Lorraine Taylor looked ready to
fall apart. Dark circles weighted her light eyes. Her brown
hair appeared uncombed. Her open coat revealed wrinkled
blue scrubs. Tattoos covered her arms and even her hands
and neck. A quick scan did not reveal any related to gangs
or prison.

Being a school resource officer did not mean that I was
a glorified security guard, as some people thought. I was a
sworn Portland police officer, covering the Wilson cluster:
Wilson High, the two middle schools, and five elementa-
ries that fed into it. With the younger kids, by and large it
was the parents I needed to concern myself with. The older

students got, the more likely it was that they were the ones getting into trouble. At Wilson, I dealt with theft, assaults, drugs, suicide attempts. Every now and then, even a student who might be thinking about shooting up the school.

And then there were extracurriculars. Community meetings. Bike fairs. We were currently working on a talent show for all of Portland Public Schools. I did whatever I could to build relationships with students and parents.

The irony was that I was close to so many kids. Just not my own son.

But that was a problem for another day. And today a student was missing.

"I need to talk to you about my daughter, Savannah," Ms. Taylor began. "She never came—"

I raised my hand, glancing meaningfully at the three students waiting in the office. They were all listening, and I knew they would be whispering about it as soon as they were back out in the hallways. Before lunch period, rumors about Savannah would be flying all over school. I motioned Ms. Taylor to follow me back to my tiny office.

Once we were behind a closed door, I said, "I understand your daughter didn't come home last night." I'd never heard of Savannah Taylor before today, but Wilson was a big school. The secretary had told me that Savannah had transferred in from out of state and that so far, she was getting good grades. And that this was the first time she had missed school.

"No, she didn't come home." Ms. Taylor blinked rapidly. "I was really hoping she might have come to school this morning, but when I called the office, they said she didn't show up. I'm afraid she might have run away."

I pulled out my notebook, thinking about the many times I'd had this conversation with parents over the years. Give it a day, maybe two, and with luck, this would all be over and the girl would be home, not much worse for wear.

But if it wasn't, things would probably get worse for Savannah Taylor. Runaways had to sustain themselves, and typically they had no money or skills at doing so. She would need a place to sleep. She needed to eat. If Savannah had left without her school-supplied transit pass, she needed a way to get around. Even if she was currently couch-surfing at a friend's, eventually she would be forced to go someplace else. Making her even more vulnerable to anyone who would want to take advantage of a teenage girl.

"Has she done this before?" I asked.

"Never."

A first-time runner. One who never skipped school. A smart girl, but maybe not the kind with street smarts.

"Does she have a boyfriend or a girlfriend she might be staying with?" At this age, a lot of family arguments were about sex or sexual orientation.

Ms. Taylor shook her head. "I don't think she's made a lot of friends here yet."

"Have you tried calling her?"

"She left her phone behind. And I can't see who she calls or texts or anything because it has a pass code and I don't know it." She paused, looked down at the tattoos on her knuckles. They read BABY DOLL. "I guess she had a fight with my boyfriend just before she left."

Left her phone. Fight with my boyfriend. My attention sharpened. Had we just gone from runaway to missing person? Or even from runaway to victim? "Were you not at home when this happened?"

"I work swing shift, and Tim—that's my boyfriend—he works days. I guess they had this . . . argument while I was at work."

"So Tim lives with you?"

"Actually, we live with him. We moved here about seven months ago."

"Have he and Savannah argued before?"

"This was the first time. They normally get along fine." As she spoke, she looked away. Had Savannah left because she didn't feel safe? Because it was in no sense "home"? Was she being abused?

"What's Tim's last name? Where does he work?"

"Hixon. And he works at Schillers Auto Repair." She hesitated, then said in a rush, "Does all that really matter?"

I kept on as if she hadn't protested. "How about Savannah's father? Could she be with him?"

"Last I heard, he was living in Texas. Savannah hasn't had any contact with him since she was two." She grimaced as if her mouth tasted sour. "And she knows that he's never paid child support."

"Is there any chance she could be suicidal?" New in town, no friends that the mom could name, father figures she couldn't trust—it wouldn't be a complete shock.

"No. Never." But Ms. Taylor's breath shook.

"Tell me more about what happened," I said.

"After she and Tim had their . . . argument, my daughter went to her kung fu class, but she never came back. And I know she was there, because I talked to the instructor this morning."

I blinked. "Kung fu? Is this the class taught by Sifu Terry?" Daniel loved Sifu Terry. He was always talking about him and about what they had learned in class. Some of the moves Daniel showed me were ones I'd tried to teach him before, but of course it wasn't as interesting when your own dad was the instructor.

Her eyes widened. "How do you know about that school?"

"Because my son Daniel takes classes there, too."

Her eyes went to the nameplate on my desk and then back to my face. "You're Daniel Diaz's father?"

"Yes." Something inside me went still. Waiting. Waiting for the rest of it.

"Sifu told me that he left while they were still mopping the floor."

"While *who* was?"

"My daughter and your son. Savannah and Daniel. The last time anyone saw her, she was with Daniel."

JENNY DOWD

I GOT UP TO USE THE BATHROOM. THE GIRL DIDN'T EVEN STIR. That worried me. But when I leaned over her, her breathing was even.

In the hallway, the light falling through the translucent vent cover let me know it was late morning. Without a phone, clock, or watch, it was so hard to keep track of time. Every day I made a tick mark on a paper napkin hidden in the back of a cupboard. But since I wasn't sure when I'd started it, I didn't really know what day of the week it was. Maybe even what month.

After I flushed the toilet, I did what I no longer allowed myself to do.

I turned on the bathroom light and looked at my face.

Or what was left of it.

I did not let myself blink. I made myself see it. Every

inch of red that still showed the marks of being stitched together.

My face was no longer a bloody, open horror.

It was worse.

I looked like a monster. Sir had taken out the stitches, but my skin was still angry, crimson and swollen, meeting in some places, gaping in others.

My bottom lip had a hole in it now. The ripped edges of my torn left nostril had also refused to knit together. I whistled when I breathed, and I drooled all the time. A barely healed gash ran from the edge of my lower eyelid nearly to my chin. A bit higher, and I would have lost my eye.

When my face started to burn, I realized I was crying, salty tears slowly leaking from my eyes. With a piece of toilet paper, I dabbed at them as lightly as I could. The pain still made me wince. Then I flipped the switch down and left. Since it was daytime, I decided it was okay to turn on the light in the bedroom. I wanted to look at her, check to see if she was okay.

Lying on her side, curled around her broken arm in its makeshift splint, the girl still didn't stir. Sir had said to let her sleep, that that would help her heal, but wasn't there a point when it was too long?

I sat back down on the edge of the bed. The girl's scraped-up face was slack, her mouth open. She was so still. Could she be dead? A fist squeezed my heart. Holding my breath, I leaned closer. Her chest was definitely moving. Her hair was dark like mine, but wavier. It smelled so sweet, like apples. I had run out of shampoo months ago, and Sir hadn't brought any more.

Even though I was only an inch away from her face, her breath kept the same rhythm and she didn't move.

With trembling fingers, I reached out and gently cupped her left hand, the injured one. She still didn't flinch or react in any way. Her fingers were the same color and temperature as mine. I released her hand. It stayed limp.

After all these lonely months, here was this girl, plopped down in the middle of my bedroom. It felt like she filled up every square inch of space. She was an alien who had crash-landed on planet Jenny. Even asleep, she changed everything. Someone else to look at. Someone else to talk to, at least once she woke up.

What would she think when she saw me? Would she scream? Throw up? The first time I saw myself in a mirror, I had gotten sick. Vomited so hard some of the stitches had ripped free.

The quilt had fallen away from the top half of her body. Her green, short-sleeve T-shirt read MO DUK PAI. I said the words out loud. I said everything out loud now, just to have someone to talk to. Occasionally I recorded myself singing and then played it back and sang the harmony. Somehow these things made me feel less alone. When a faint frown creased her face, I realized I needed to remember how I had behaved out in the world. I went into the living area. Sir had left the backpack on the couch, so it must be hers. I looked inside. There wasn't much. A wallet, a big library book about that kung fu guy Bruce Lee, and a black cloth sash that I figured must have something to do with the book.

The wallet held three dollars. A little pocket that

fastened with a snap held two quarters and a nickel. In the slots for cards, there were just three: a library card, a driver's license, and a student ID for Wilson High. Her name was Savannah Taylor, and she was a sophomore.

Maybe it was a good thing Savannah was still asleep. Now that I saw the RV through her eyes, it seemed cluttered and not all that clean. Some of it I couldn't help, like the stains on the carpet and built-in chairs. But I could at least straighten up.

Trying to be as quiet as possible, I started putting away the clothes I had washed earlier in the kitchen sink, even though they weren't quite dry. To make things neater, I put things into piles. Then I balled up a paper towel, wet it in the kitchen sink, and began to swipe at the cobwebs in the corners.

When I first realized that I was stuck here forever, stuck in a space I could cross in nine paces, I almost went crazy. The silence lay heavy in my ears. No one to talk to, nothing to look at. My friends, my family, the freedom to go anyplace in my car—all of it had been taken away as if it had never been. It was like living in a cave, with only my sounds to fill the space. I talked and sang to myself, but it didn't make any difference. I was all alone, my thoughts pawing at me, day after day, night after night.

I slept as much as possible. It helped me escape the pain of my face. And it made it so that I could return to the outside world, even just in my dreams. Time folded in on itself and then stretched out endlessly. A day could be the same as an hour, or an hour the same as a day.

Some days I felt nothing but small. Others I felt

enormous, the RV shrinking around me. I couldn't turn without knocking over something. Whenever Sir came by, I would tremble with fear. But it was also a strange relief to know that I was not alone in the world.

When Savannah woke up, she would have to deal with the same reality I had so many months ago. But at least she wouldn't have to deal with it alone.

DANIEL DIAZ

I HAD NEVER BEEN SUMMONED OUT OF CLASS TO GO TO THE office before. What was even weirder was that once I got there, the school secretary said my *dad* needed to talk to me.

My dad and me had kind of an unspoken agreement. At school, we acted like I wasn't his kid and he wasn't my dad.

A dark-haired lady with lots of tattoos was sitting in the waiting area. I didn't know her, but something about her was familiar. She seemed to be staring at me, but maybe that was because by now I was also looking at her, trying to place where I'd seen those blue eyes before.

I knocked once on the door to my dad's small office, then pushed it open. Maybe no one else would have noticed, but his normal poker face was showing cracks. It was in the way his eyes turned down at the corners, how he pressed his lips together. Something was definitely wrong.

I stopped in the doorway. I wasn't going to take another step until he told me what was up. "Did something happen to Mom?" My voice broke, but I didn't care. "Or Orlando?" Orlando was my younger brother.

"What? No!" Dad sounded impatient. "They're both fine." He blew air through pursed lips. "Just come in and close the door behind you."

I did, but I didn't sit down. "What's up?" I still couldn't read the emotion leaking out of him. Was he mad? Scared? And what did it have to do with me? I couldn't think of anything I'd done wrong.

"Just sit down, Daniel." His tone was impatient. "Sit down and tell me what you did last night."

"Last night? I went to kung fu, came home, took a shower, had dinner, ate some ice cream, did my homework. Then I played video games and went to bed." Dad had been at a community meeting, so he hadn't been home for much if any of that. Having a dad who was a cop meant he might not be there for a kung fu tournament, a birthday party, or even Christmas morning. Ironically, we saw each other more at school than we did at home.

When I was a little kid, it had been cool to have a cop for a dad. I could bring him on career day or even for show-and-tell. Looking at him in his uniform made me feel so much pride.

As I got older, it became slightly more complicated. I started noticing how cautious my dad was and how little he trusted anyone but himself. He was always grilling me and Orlando and even my mom. Whenever me or my brother made a new friend, the joke was that before we could even think of going over to visit, my dad had to know the full legal name and date of birth of everyone who lived in the house. All my friends were allowed to go to birthday parties or the mall by themselves years before me.

My dad had taught me a lot of things. Not to trust strangers. To always treat a gun like it was loaded. That most people didn't understand what it was like to be a cop. (He ruined any TV show or movie with a cop in it, complaining loudly about how wrong they got everything.)

And because my dad was a cop, people expected me to be either a narc or a rebel—as if there weren't any in-betweens.

He was the one who got me into kung fu, way back in third grade. He wanted me to know how to defend myself. But lately whenever I talked about Sifu Terry or even Bruce Lee, he looked impatient.

Now he said, "Tell me more about what happened at kung fu class."

"It was just a regular class. We did grab counters." The whole time I was talking, my anxiety was increasing. "Why? What's wrong?"

He jerked his chin in the direction of the door. "That's Savannah Taylor's mom out there. She said Savannah never came home last night. And she's not at school today."

"What? But her mom picked her up after class."

My dad's thick eyebrows drew together. "The mom couldn't have picked her up. She works swing shift. And Sifu Terry told her that you two closed up the dojo together."

Did my dad think I was hiding Savannah someplace?

"Are you asking if I know where Savannah is? Because I don't."

"I'm just trying to gather information. What made you think her mom was picking her up? Did you see Savannah getting into a car?"

"I asked if I could walk her home. She said her mom was waiting for her in the upper parking lot. Why would she lie to me about that?"

"Maybe she was meeting someone else up there. Does she have a friend she might be with?"

I thought of the times I had noticed Savannah at lunch, always with a book. "I haven't seen her talking with anyone else at school. She just moved here last summer. All I know is that she was upset when she came to class. She looked like she'd been crying. And she said something about a fight with her mom's boyfriend. I think his name is Tim."

My dad leaned forward. "What did she say about him?"

"I don't remember exactly. Something about how Tim said it was stupid for her to take kung fu."

"Tim told Savannah's mom about the argument. He said the last he saw of her was when she left for class." Dad tapped his lips with his index finger. "Do you think she might have run away rather than go back home?"

"No." I shook my head.

"Why are you so sure?"

"If she was running away, why would she bother to go to kung fu first?"

My dad shrugged. "Teens can be impulsive. Maybe she started walking home and realized she didn't want to face him."

"She *was* upset," I said slowly. "And she definitely didn't like that Tim guy. She might even have been afraid of him."

My dad considered this. A muscle flexed in his jaw. "Do you think he was hurting her?" The specifics of *hurting* hung unspoken in the air.

"I don't know. Maybe." Why had I been so focused on myself last night, instead of on her? The inside of my nose started to sting as I followed things to their logical conclusion. "Dad—do you think he did something to Savannah?"

TIM HIXON

WHEN THE COP, SOME GUY NAMED DIAZ, SAID "YOUR STEP-daughter," I stopped him. We were standing outside my work bay. Next to us, a Dodge Ramcharger hung suspended, waiting for me to figure out what was making the strange noise its owner could not describe in any way that made sense.

Savannah was Lorraine's daughter. She had nothing to do with me. And that was by her choice.

I had tried to be friendly. But she never liked me, not from the get-go. She was always shooting her mom a look or rolling her eyes when I talked. As if I wasn't right there.

I knew how to recognize disrespect.

That girl had no idea how good she had it. Had I ever laid a finger on her? No. Not even when she was just asking for a spanking. And no matter what some people might think, she wasn't too big for that. You were never too big, not when you insisted on talking back. Insisted on acting like a spoiled brat.

And she was spoiled. I'd even let her have her own room, put my motorcycle outside, let her and Lorraine paint it this pinky-purple color called "Violets in the Spring."

When I was a kid, I slept on a couch. Never had my own bedroom. And that didn't hurt me one bit. If anything, it made me stronger.

The cop kept badgering me. "Why didn't you report your girlfriend's daughter's disappearance right away?"

"What disappearance? She left for that karate class she takes." I knew it was kung fu, but it felt good to call it karate.

"But she didn't come back. Why didn't you alert her mother at work? Why didn't you call the police?"

"I figured Savannah was just mad at me, but I knew she'd come back eventually. I mean, where else was she going to go? And by the time Lorraine came home, I was already asleep. She didn't say nothing. I thought Savannah must have come back." This morning, Lorraine had been hysterical. But I wasn't worried. Savannah was probably just being stubborn.

That girl didn't even know how lucky she was to be getting a free ride. When I was her age, I was working thirty-six hours a week at a TacoTime. I was a shift manager, and proud of it. A sixteen-year-old shift manager.

And I didn't have any adults to live with. My mom was living with a friend. My stepdad had moved out before she did. Which was one way of saying he was in Multnomah County Jail awaiting trial.

My little sister was in foster care. My mom had kicked me out for telling the school counselor what my stepdad was doing to my sister.

I'm the one who betrayed him.

When he was the only dad I'd ever known.

And it turned out that nobody was happier and nothing got better.

After everything went to hell, I wished I'd kept my mouth shut. But I'd seen how my sister cried. And then how she closed herself off.

Since I didn't want to go into foster care, I disappeared when the social workers came around. At sixteen, I had to figure out how to make it on my own. If I didn't work enough hours, I didn't eat, except for mistakes. And when the owner is watching you like a hawk, you have to be careful about making mistakes on purpose. Something had to give. And what gave was school.

But Savannah got to go every day. She'd already had more schooling than me. And she had lots of opinions, which she was more than happy to share.

"You've already admitted that you argued that night. Is there anything else that happened that you want to tell me about, Tim?"

There was no way they were going to pin this on me. "No."

The cop shook his head, looking grave. "You've had a DWI."

"Only once. It was a mistake, and I took a class." It had been tough not driving, even if it was only for a few weeks. My car was a real classic. A 1968 Camaro. Right now it was parked on the back lot, waiting for the increasingly rare parts it needed to be shipped.

The car had belonged to my stepdad. When he went to prison, he gave it to me.

The thing was, I actually liked him. How messed up was that? But he was the closest thing I ever had to a father. He even took me fishing. He showed me how to tie knots, how to cast the line, how to gut the fish.

Using the knife he handed me, I followed his instructions on how to split open the white belly. I wanted to throw up, but I didn't. I just swallowed hard and pushed the sick feeling back down.

I was good at that.

I ignored the way the flat silver eye of the fish stared at me. The way the white flesh resisted. And then parted. The way its tail wiggled back and forth as I sawed. He said it was just from the knife. I kept doing what he said. Holding the head between two fingers, sticking the fingers of my other hand into the slit I'd made. It felt like I was putting my fingers into a mouth. I pulled out the red and pink and white guts and dropped them into the water.

And I didn't feel a thing.

Now the cop took a step closer. "And what about that other arrest, Tim? The one for domestic violence?"

To see a thing uncolored by one's own personal preferences and desires is to see it in its own pristine simplicity.

—BRUCE LEE

SAVANNAH TAYLOR

MY FIRST CONSCIOUS THOUGHT WASN'T MADE UP OF WORDS. Instead, it was a silent scream. It felt like it had been echoing inside me for an eternity.

I had to move, to get up, to run. Had to get away. I no longer knew from what, just that I would surely die if I didn't.

But as I started to push myself upright, pain even stronger than my terror ripped through me. I slumped back with a groan.

"It's okay," a girl's voice said. A gentle hand patted my shoulder. "You're safe."

The events that had brought me here slowly filtered into my memory. When I had tried to run in the parking lot, I had fallen, hit my head, and passed out, which meant I probably had a concussion. And I hadn't improved things by leaping out of a van while it was moving. Now my wrist throbbed, my head pulsed in time with my heart, and my ribs hurt when I took a breath.

"Where is he?" The words came out slurred. *Wear see?* My tongue felt like a piece of leather.

"Don't worry," said the girl. I could tell she was sitting next to me, on the edge of the bed where I lay under the covers. "It's just you and me. But we should be quiet. He doesn't like noise."

Finally I forced open my heavy lids. I was in a dimly lit room. The double bed filled the small space nearly edge to edge. Short brown curtains covered the windows.

Wincing, I slowly turned my head to look the girl in the eye. And shrieked.

She looked like Frankenstein's monster, if he were a teenaged girl. Barely healed scars crisscrossed her face. The edges of a torn nostril didn't quite meet, and there was a red hole in the middle of her lower lip.

The girl didn't flinch, but steadily met my gaze with her blue eyes. Her eyes and her forehead were the only untouched parts of her face. With the back of her hand, she wiped her wet-looking chin.

"What happened to you?"

"A dog bit me."

My own face hurt. Suddenly fearful, I tried to bring up my hands to touch it, but found my left arm was in a makeshift splint. I frantically ran my right hand over my forehead, eyelids, cheeks, nose, and chin. While parts felt scraped and bruised, my features seemed whole.

"I'm Jenny," she said as I pawed at my face. "And you're Savannah, right?"

Hearing my name come out of a stranger's mouth sent another zap of adrenaline through me. "How do you know my name?"

"Sorry. I went through the wallet in your backpack." Jenny's straight dark hair fell past her shoulders. Under a gray cardigan, she was wearing skinny jeans and a tight red sweater with a deep V-neck. She leaned closer. "He took me, too." Her whisper was as light as a breath.

"We have to get out of here." But where was *here*? My best guess was some tiny shack in the woods, but that still didn't seem quite right.

Jenny shook her head. "You need to rest. You're hurt."

For an answer, I threw back the covers and pushed myself up with my good hand. I swung my legs over the edge of the bed, ignoring how the room tilted. When I steadied myself on the ivory-colored wall, it felt cool and oddly slick. The wall was made of plastic.

I went to the window, with Jenny trailing behind me. But when I pushed aside the curtain, all I saw was flat silver. At first I thought it was paint, but then I realized the window had been covered from the outside with a shiny plastic tarp.

Increasingly light-headed, I made for the doorway, ignoring Jenny telling me to stop, to come back.

I staggered down the short hall. When the elbow of my bad arm banged against the wall, pain turned the edges of my vision white. I passed a tiny bathroom with a half-open folding door. This wasn't a shack, I realized. It was a motor home.

As the space opened out into a carpeted living area,

Jenny grabbed my shoulder. With a twist, I shook her hand loose and made for the door in the far wall. Its window was also covered. I grabbed the handle.

"Don't open that!" Jenny said urgently behind me.

I turned the handle and pushed. It started to open, revealing a sliver of light. Cold air rushed in through the crack. Metal rattled. I was already moving my foot to step outside when the door's movement abruptly stopped. The gap was only about three inches wide. In frustration, I bashed the door with my shoulder, ignoring how it set off echoes of pain. But the door refused to budge.

Putting my eye to the gap, I caught a glimpse of a heavy metal chain that was preventing it from opening all the way. Below it was dark, muddy ground. "Help! Help us!" I shouted through the gap.

Suddenly the door vibrated under my palm when something scrabbled and scratched at the metal. And in the gap I saw a dark and terrible eye, a monster's eye with no white at all.

It tried to thrust its head in farther, just below my face. A growl filled the room. With a shriek, I pulled back. The dog's mouth snapped open and closed, black-rimmed lips stretched over long white teeth. Silvery threads of saliva bound together the top and bottom canines.

Jenny pushed me away with one hand while she wrenched the door closed with the other. Outside, the dog began to bark, angry and urgent.

"I told you not to do that!" She brought her hands to her stitched-together face. Her nails were ragged, bitten to the quick. "Did Rex bite you?"

The adrenaline and fear that had propelled me this far suddenly disappeared. I fell more than sat on the small couch. "No."

She scurried to the window, bent down, and pressed one eye to it. There was the tiniest of gaps at the bottom where the tarp had slipped. "If Sir hears Rex, he'll come back, and he'll be so mad. He hates noise."

"We have to get out of here."

"Even if we got out of here, we won't get past Rex. I already tried to escape, months ago." Turning back to me, she gestured at her ruined face. "And you can see how far that got me."

"You said that guy took you, too. When was that?"

"Back in February."

But this was December. Jenny had been here for months and months. Nearly a year. The feeling of the room closing in, of the edges of my vision dimming, crashed back over me like a sneaker wave.

BLAKE DOWD

"TWO WEEKS UNTIL CHRISTMAS BREAK," IAN SAID AS HE handed me a red Solo cup. "I cannot wait."

I nodded as I took the beer. School was mostly torture, because it meant staying still, and I was terrible at that. But being home would not be any better. I headed to the back of the basement and leaned against the wall, on the edge of the party but not really part of it.

Thanksgiving had been bad enough, but at least that had been only four days. Lately my mom was either at work or sitting silently on the couch, a glass of wine in her hand, staring at nothing. My dad hadn't lived with us since the summer, when they argued about him buying presents for Jenny's birthday. And whenever I was at home, I was hyperaware of Jenny's room lying empty, like a rotting cavity hidden deep in a mouth.

I was the one that lived. Did my parents ever regret that? Jenny had always been the easy one. Pretty. Obedient. Smart.

Now Jenny was gone. And not gone.

My mom was sure she was dead. My dad was sure she was alive. And me? I felt like Jenny was stuck. Both living and dead, like Schrödinger's cat.

My friend Ian, who was way smarter than me, had told me about this physicist, this Schrödinger guy, who had created something that was called a thought experiment. It imagined that you put a cat, a Geiger counter, a bottle of hydrochloric acid, and a tiny bit of radioactive material into a steel box.

Geiger counters detect radioactive emissions, and the second this imaginary Geiger counter detected even a single atom decaying, it was set to trip a hammer that would shatter the bottle of poison, which would kill the cat.

So sooner or later, in the thought experiment, the cat would die. You just didn't know when. Some physicists believed that after a while, the cat would be simultaneously alive and dead—at least until someone opened the steel box to look. Of course once you looked, the cat could only be alive or dead, not both.

Jenny was the cat, but she was still inside the box. Unobserved. So she was both dead *and* alive.

All around me, kids were laughing and talking. A few people were dancing, and a few more were making out. Ian was walking around with a sprig of mistletoe over his head, trying to get girls to kiss him.

Just like Schrödinger's cat, just like Jenny, I was here and not here.

Christmas Day would probably be a repeat of Thanksgiving, only worse, because it was Christmas. My grandma was again insisting that the whole family get together. She would make food that no one in my immediate family would do more than push around their plates. My uncle would "share" Bible verses about God's plans and the afterlife, while my aunt laid her hand on his arm and whispered at him to stop. Their little girls would run around, high on sugar cookies, while my mom watched them, her face a mask. Looking like if you touched it, it would crack and then crumble into dust.

If we followed the pattern laid down by Thanksgiving, my dad, allowed home only for the holiday, would talk too much and drink even more than that. Then he and my mom would end up in Jenny's room, shouting at each other before he stormed out.

My parents weren't divorced yet, but my dad had moved to a ratty apartment building and spent all his free time searching for Jenny.

By now she would have been away at college. Probably getting straight As.

The night Jenny disappeared from Island Tan, my mom kept calling her cell after she didn't come home, but my sister didn't pick up. My dad's the one who drove out there and found the place unlocked, all lit up, her car parked in front. Both the bank deposit and Jenny were gone. Later, the police checked the security footage from the bank, but the ATM camera didn't reach far enough to show what happened to her. To show who had taken her, or if she had left with someone else.

Our whole life turned upside down. Home became where the craziness was. For weeks, our house was full of people. Cops, neighbors, my parents' friends, reporters.

At first having cops at our house made me feel safe. But it wasn't long before I got tired of them answering our landline, drinking out of our coffee cups, and never, ever leaving. I couldn't walk around in my boxers anymore, because I might run into a police officer or even a reporter. Once I wandered out into the living room in my pajama bottoms and my parents were on the couch, lit up by bright lights on black metal stands, doing an interview for the evening news.

Just like with the cops, initially it was kind of cool, having people I'd only ever seen on TV in my house. They acted like they just wanted to help. They were friendly. Sympathetic. But as time went on, the reporters asked awful questions, like did I think Jenny was being sexually abused. Or they ran stories that turned out way different than I'd thought. I learned there was no such thing as "off the record." Eventually I figured out that their real priority wasn't finding my sister, but getting people to watch their shows.

After the first week came and went with no Jenny, my parents told me things had to get back to normal. That I had to go back to school. But things there weren't back to normal either. Some kids acted like having a missing sister was contagious. And some acted like I was a celebrity. They even asked for my autograph.

At home, I felt like a ghost. You would have thought my parents would have been all over me, putting tracking software on my phone, insisting that I call them whenever I went someplace new. Instead, they barely seemed to notice me. After Jenny disappeared, I started eating dinner at Ian's house and slept there most nights. Eventually, it was Ian's parents who started getting uncomfortable with how much time I spent there, who started encouraging me to go home.

Instead, I just found other people to hang out with. All I wanted to do was drink beer and not talk about Jenny. When I was with my friends, it was easier not to think. Not to think about all the times I had yelled at Jenny, told her to get out of my room, out of my face, out of my life.

And then all of a sudden, she was.

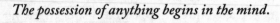

The possession of anything begins in the mind.

—BRUCE LEE

SAVANNAH TAYLOR

OUTSIDE, THE DOG WAS STILL BARKING FURIOUSLY. TREMBLING, I surveyed the living/dining area. In addition to the couch, it also held two swivel chairs, one of which faced a built-in table with a fixed bench on the other side. At the back, a floor-to-ceiling curtain hid what was presumably the driving area. Everything was made of polyester and plastic in the exact same strange shade of flat brown.

On the table sat a few magazines and books, as well as an old-fashioned silver boom box, with a half dozen CDs and cassette tapes stacked next to it. In my rush to get out, I hadn't noticed the heaps of plastic boxes and bags mounded along the walls. They made the small space feel even more cramped.

I tried to take slow, deep breaths, like Sifu had taught us in kung fu, but they didn't go very far.

Jenny stood with her arms wrapped around herself. "You just better hope that Sir doesn't get mad and come back with the Taser."

"To use on us or the dog?"

She raised an eyebrow. "What do you think?" Outside, the dog's barks were gradually slowing down.

I thought back to what had happened in the upper parking lot. "Before he took me, all of a sudden, it felt like all my muscles tightened up, and I fell over. Is that what happened?"

Jenny nodded. "It shoots out these two darts. If both of them hit you, it makes a circuit that sends electricity through you. That messes up your muscles and nerves so you can't even stand. But he can also press the end of it against you for a direct shock. That way doesn't lock up your muscles—it just hurts like hell. Even more than being hit by the darts. And the longer he holds it against you, the worse it is." Wincing, she rubbed her neck. "You don't ever want to make him mad."

"He must have used those darts on me. I got knocked out when I fell down."

"That's why he wanted you to rest. He said you might have a concussion from hitting your head. But being conscious when he does it is not really an improvement. You can't move, you can't think."

She was clearly speaking from experience. With every word, it felt more and more like I was suffocating, like the walls of this tiny room were closing in. The air smelled of mold and dust, oil and cigarettes. It smelled like the man who had taken me.

But did it also smell like Tim?

"What's this guy's real name? Is it Tim? Tim Hixon?"

Jenny shrugged one shoulder. "I don't know. He doesn't let me call him anything but Sir. And you'd better always call him Sir, or he'll tase you too."

"What does he look like?"

"Blue eyes. Balding. Bigger than me. Older. Maybe forty?"

Every word she said fit Tim. But my excitement dissipated even before it built. Because it was also kind of a generic description. If a guy shaved his head, you wouldn't even know what color his hair was. And how many guys had blue eyes and were over forty?

The description also fit Mr. Tae Kwan Do, the guy from class who thought he didn't deserve to be last in line. I didn't know much about him, other than his moods ranged from annoyed to angry, and that he punched way too hard whenever we sparred. Had he watched me leave, night after night, and then decided the upper lot would be a perfect place to take me?

But Mr. Tae Kwan Do and Tim weren't the only men I knew who resembled Jenny's description. A couple of teachers at Wilson looked like that, as well as probably half a dozen random guys I crossed paths with each week. And what about Mr. Fryer, the dad whose five-year-old twins I babysat every couple of weeks? When he paid me, he always stood too close, and when he drove me home, he asked questions that made me uncomfortable. Once he had even asked if I had a boyfriend, which seemed a weird question for a married forty-year-old guy to ask a sixteen-year-old girl.

"I'm just trying to figure out if I know him. He came up on me from behind. I never saw his face, and I only heard him swear. Is there anything else distinctive about him? Is he overweight or skinny, or does he have a scar or tattoos?"

"He's the kind of guy you wouldn't look at twice." Jenny's laugh sounded rusty. "You certainly wouldn't look at him and think he liked to kidnap girls and hold them hostage in motor homes." She pressed her ruined lips together and then said, "So who's Tim?"

"My mom's current boyfriend. He shaves his head, and he's got blue eyes. And the way you're describing Sir, it sounds like Tim." I remembered the rage in his eyes when he had accused me of sassing him, of talking back. Maybe kidnapping a girl and forcing her to call him Sir was his dream come true.

"Sir looks like a million guys." Jenny waved one hand dismissively.

Suddenly I remembered the conversation—had it only been yesterday?—at the cafeteria table about a girl who had been kidnapped. "Hey, were you working at a tanning salon when you got taken?"

Her eyes went wide. "Yeah. Island Tan. I think he thought we were going to play house. That I was going to be his perfect girl." She smiled her torn smile. "But then I had to go and spoil everything."

"What happened?" I asked.

She took a deep breath. Her eyes filled with tears as she began to speak.

JENNY DOWD

MY WORDS CAME IN FITS AND STARTS AS I DESCRIBED THAT last night to Savannah. The last normal night of my life. I tried not to think about it very often. It wasn't a night I wanted to relive.

I'd been in Island Tan's tiny office, getting ready to close up, when the front door buzzer sounded. I groaned in annoyance. I'd already cleaned all the tanning beds and the spray-tan station. I'd counted the money and put it with a deposit slip in the black zippered bank bag. When I left, I would drop it in the night deposit at the bank next door. But since it wasn't quite nine o'clock, technically we were still open for business.

When I opened the office door, I was surprised to find a middle-aged guy at the counter. Most of our clientele were teenage girls.

But Sir looked boring and safe. That was, if you even noticed him. He was easy to ignore.

Later, after he took me and I had nothing to do but think, I remembered that I'd actually seen him several times before that last day. Seen him, but never paid attention. In the car next to mine at Safeway. Parked along a route I ran almost every day. I even realized he'd come into the tanning salon on a busy evening a week earlier, disappearing before I had a chance to wait on him.

He was scanning the walls. I thought he was looking at the posters listing our prices and specials. Maybe getting ready to buy our ten-tans-for-the-price-of-eight package for his wife or daughter. So they'd be ready for winter formal or a beach vacation.

Now I knew he was really looking one last time for a camera.

There wasn't one.

Without saying a word, he took something from behind his back and pointed it at me. It looked like a gun from a science fiction movie. Plastic, chunky, black and yellow. I didn't know whether to be afraid of it.

Still I lifted my hands in the air, feeling like I was play-acting. Like this couldn't be real. "I already cleaned out the till. You can have the bank deposit. It's in the office."

"That's not what I want," he said.

As I realized what he meant, my blood turned to ice. Could I scramble back into the office and slam the door closed? Did it even lock? In my panic, I couldn't remember. Could I get to my cell phone and call 9-1-1 before he hurt me?

And then he pulled the gun's trigger. Immediately, I felt two stings, one in my chest and the other in my left arm.

My head jerked back, and my legs stiffened. I didn't remember falling, just being on the flat gray carpet, the current scrambling my thoughts and nerves.

He slipped behind the counter, leaned down, and hit me twice on the head with the side of the gun, which was just as hard and unyielding as a real gun. Later I learned it was actually a Taser. He yanked up my wrists and duct taped them together. Despite his claim that he didn't want the money, he darted into the office and came back with the black deposit bag as well as my purse. Then he yanked me to my feet. Half supporting me, he marched me into the cold night.

Only Muchos Tacos, on the far side of the strip mall, was still open. But when I managed to loll my head in its direction, I didn't see a single patron inside. The only cars on this side of the lot were my old Mazda 323 and a dirty, windowless white van. When I realized that was where he was taking me, I tried to drag my feet.

"Come on," he growled. When I still resisted, he pressed the end of the Taser against the side of my neck. My muscles didn't spasm, but the pain sucked every other thought from my head. I couldn't even scream, only whimper. But God help me, after that I willingly crawled into the back of the van. Anything to make it stop.

As I did, he slapped another piece of duct tape over my mouth. A second later, the rear door closed. And then he got in the front and drove me away.

I lay in the back, screaming into the sealed space of

my mouth. I was in no way ready to die, but I feared I would smother because it was harder and harder to breathe through my nose, stuffy from crying. The thought began to loop through my mind that that might be for the best. Because it was clear that nothing good was going to happen to me whenever he opened the van door again.

I wasn't sure how long he drove. The last bit was slow and rough, like he was maneuvering over broken ground, not a road.

Finally, the van stopped. I heard him get out. He was yelling at someone in a hard language I couldn't understand. He sounded angry. Then he opened the van's back door. My eyes had adjusted to the blackness. It was a clear night. The stars were like holes punched in the sky. A full moon, like a closed eye, hung over a wall of compacted cars.

The wall of crushed cars wasn't a straight line, but rather a ring surrounding a muddy open space. The space held me, him, the van, a ramshackle house, and an old tan motor home. The RV's windows were covered by giant silver tarps.

There was also a dog. A huge black dog that whispered a growl, low in its chest. Sir flung a guttural *Bleib!* over his shoulder, and the dog quieted. But its eyes never left me.

Holding my arm, he marched me forward toward the motor home. I turned my head. There was a narrow gap in the wall of smashed cars, a gap he had driven through. Past the gap were rows and rows of junked cars. Some so old trees were growing through them. And past all the cars, I caught a glimpse of a chain-wire fence.

"I think we're in the back of a junkyard," I told Savannah now. "Like a wrecking yard for old cars. And of course a junkyard needs a junkyard dog. Rex just roams around, probably to stop anyone who might be thinking about stealing parts. But he also stops us from getting out."

With her head, Savannah gestured at the door. Rex had finally stopped barking. "Is that the same dog who bit you? The one that just tried to get in?"

I nodded, remembering how Sir had let go of me so that he could fit a key in a padlock. The lock held the ends of a metal chain he had bolted to either side of the door. Once he put me inside and fastened the lock, I would not be able to get out.

"I tried to run before he even put me in here. But my wrists were duct taped together. I only made it about a hundred yards before Rex got me. He could have killed me. And he almost did."

I fell silent, remembering. Sprinting across the muddy ground toward that gap. Not really knowing where I was going, just that I was.

And then ahead of me was the dog. He crouched, gathering himself to leap. Time slowed down. His jaws were wide open, aimed right at my throat. I tucked my chin.

I protected my throat from Rex with the only other thing I had to offer him: my face.

BOB DOWD

THE YOUNG WOMAN CURLED UP IN THE SLEEPING BAG UNDER-neath the overpass, next to a brindled pit bull, had dark hair and pale skin. My breath caught.

As it had dozens of times before.

Still, I circled around to look at her face. She was young, probably still a teenager.

But she wasn't Jenny.

She wasn't my daughter.

Even several feet away, I could smell her. There's a certain smell of homelessness. It's not pee. It's just living in the same clothes. It's not even an unpleasant smell.

The girl's eyes flew open, and she pushed herself up on one elbow. The dog bared its teeth at me.

"I'm just looking for this girl." I held out the flyer with three photos of Jenny. Two were real and one had been generated by a special software program that showed her with her hair chopped off and her face gaunt. The police had released it to the media on the six-month anniversary of her disappearance, figuring that if she was still alive, by now she might look nothing like the smiling, healthy Jenny in our original photos. For a few weeks, I got messages on the Facebook page I'd set up. Even though nothing panned out, it was still comforting. Our daughter hadn't been forgotten.

"She's about your age." Would Jenny even recognize me now? I'd lost thirty pounds. How could I eat if I didn't know if she was being fed? My hair was threaded with gray. How could I sleep if she might not be able to? Technically, I still wrote software manuals, but finding Jenny had become my real job.

When the police stopped actively searching for her, it felt like my heart was being ripped out. What if she was still out there, hurting, in trouble? But in their eyes, she had probably been kidnapped and killed. A few people floated the theory that she had taken the bank deposit and run, but that didn't explain why she had left her car behind, why her phone hadn't pinged once since that night.

But I couldn't give up on her. What if some creep had taken her and then let her go when he got tired of her? Or if she had really stolen the money, she might have decided we had written her off. Either way, she could be too ashamed to contact us.

So every weekend and most weeknights, I searched for her. Truck stops. The Greyhound station. Malls. Parks. Strip clubs. Homeless shelters. The Amtrak station. Under bridges. By the river. In front of convenience stores.

I knew what people thought. That I was denying the reality Jenny was gone for good. More than likely dead. That it was just a way to stave off pain and grief.

But it was far from a blessing to believe—to know—Jenny was alive. Because that meant she must be going through something that I couldn't even imagine.

At times I even wished that they would find Jenny's body. Maybe then I could have worked toward the closure that the two therapists I'd seen talked about. I would have a grave where I could visit my beautiful daughter and mourn.

Now the homeless girl covered the dog's snout with one hand and took the piece of paper with the other. *Missing: Jenny Dowd* it said at the top. It listed the day she went missing, her birth date, her brown hair and blue eyes, the scar she had on one knee, her lack of tattoos.

Jenny's disappearance had broken open my beliefs about the world and revealed them for the lies they were. Lies about how bad things only happened to other people. About how things always turned out okay in the end.

The girl in the sleeping bag looked from the flyer to me. "Is this your daughter?"

I nodded, feeling ashamed. When you're a father, you only have one duty, and I had failed. I hadn't protected my child.

After Jenny disappeared, some people looked at my family with suspicion. How could a girl vanish so completely? Unless one of us was lying about what had happened. And of the three of us, it was me they side-eyed the most. I would have been just one of a long line of husbands, boyfriends, fathers, and stepfathers who had gone on TV and cried and begged for their missing loved ones to be returned. We all knew how those stories ended. With the sobbing man revealed as the guilty party.

"Yeah," I told the girl. "Have you seen her? Or anyone who looks like her?"

In the first few weeks after Jenny disappeared, when the media was still interested in us, people reported seeing her walking in San Francisco's Golden Gate Park. Shopping at Hot Topic in Omaha. They caught a glimpse of her in a back room of a strip club in Boise.

Only it was never her, or by the time word reached us, it was weeks or months later. Still, I had chased after leads, used up all my vacation time. Nearly every day there was a sighting that had to be followed up, just in case it was real. Jenny could still be somewhere, wanting to come home. Maybe putting up one more flyer, calling one more senator, begging one more reporter to write a story, maybe that would make a difference.

But now I wondered if they would even be interested on the anniversary.

How long can a person live on hope?

Amy said it wasn't even hope anymore, just stubbornness. I said that people were taking their cues from us, and that if they saw us giving up on her, they would too. Amy said that I had never been good at accepting reality, and this was just more proof. She believed Jenny must have died that first night.

Amy made that choice because otherwise she would go crazy.

But I didn't believe Jenny was dead. Just like I didn't believe that our marriage was. Sure, we fought a lot, but yelling at each other and throwing things was an escape valve when we were both on the verge of exploding.

Then Amy had said one of us had to leave. That she couldn't live with my searching anymore. That she had to move on.

So I moved out. Moved out but not on. And we hadn't yet filed the paperwork to get divorced.

My apartment complex was filled with single mothers, old people trying to stretch their Social Security checks, and other men who had suddenly found themselves alone. Like me.

Amy had started volunteering for In Trevor's Memory. She helped other parents whose children were missing.

But when we were the ones with a missing child, we hadn't been able to help each other.

The girl in the sleeping bag looked from one photo of Jenny to the next.

Every couple of months, a news story reinforced my belief that she was alive. A girl, missing for three years, found in a hidden basement room. A boy who went to the police after his longtime captor took another boy. A girl who swam across a lake after being held captive for months in a ramshackle cabin.

When I was a kid, my grandma would make these truly awful Jell-O desserts, pieces of canned fruit suspended in crayon-colored jelly. I felt like that. Suspended, unnatural, unable to move.

Sometimes girls I met on the street would claim that

they thought they'd seen Jenny, at least long enough to get coffee and a hot meal in a restaurant that couldn't shoo them out because they were now a paying customer.

But this girl was honest. She looked up and said, "I don't think so."

I focused on her for a second. She wasn't my daughter, but she was still someone's child. "You should go to a shelter. It's not safe out here for you. Even with your dog."

"But I can't go to a shelter. *Because* of my dog." I could see the girl mentally cataloging my dirty tennis shoes, my jeans worn to threads at the heels. "But if you give me five bucks, I'll hold on to this flyer. And I'll keep an eye out. For Jenny."

Even knowing it was probably a lie, I took out my wallet.

Because what if this girl was the key? The key to finding my daughter.

To hell with circumstances; I create opportunities.

—BRUCE LEE

SAVANNAH TAYLOR

SLUMPED IN ONE OF THE RV'S SWIVEL CHAIRS, JENNY TOLD ME about the night the man she called Sir had taken her. The whole time she was speaking, her fingertips absently traced the red ridges of her face.

"So we're in a wrecking yard?"

"Yeah, there are lots of junked cars." With the back of her hand, she wiped her glistening chin, wet with leaking spit.

I averted my eyes. "My mom's boyfriend is named Tim Hixon. He's a mechanic. And he drives this stupid old 1968 Camaro that's always breaking down. A couple of times he even made us go with him to some nasty old junkyard to see if they had the parts he needed."

Jenny straightened up. "Do you think he's the one who took me? Who took us?"

"It kind of makes sense, at least as much sense as

anything does. He hates if you question him. He calls it disrespectful and talking back. And he goes out at night a lot when my mom's at work. She works swing shift. He never says where he's going. Maybe he's been coming here to see you." This motor home, the tiny stained couch I was sitting on, the scarred girl sitting across from me, my broken wrist splinted with a magazine—it was hard to believe any of it was real. I was trying not to look at her face, but it was impossible not to. "Who stitched you up?" I asked.

"Sir did. Whoever he is. He watched prepper videos on YouTube on his phone. Of course, they're about how to do surgery if society collapses. Not how to stitch up some girl you're holding hostage." She grimaced. "Before he started, he had me drink a bunch of whiskey, almost to the point of passing out."

Whiskey. Tim mostly drank beer, but he kept a bottle of whiskey on top of our fridge.

As I replayed the rest of what she had said, my stomach did a slow flip. How much would it hurt to have someone sew your *face*? "Almost?"

Her torn lips twisted. "Yeah, it probably would have been better if I had. He kept yelling at me to stop moving. He drank a lot, too. You could tell the whole thing was really grossing him out."

"Oh my God." I didn't want to imagine it, but my brain kept showing me pictures anyway. "So this guy, has he . . ." My voice trailed off. "Has he left you alone?" I tried to take a deep breath, but it didn't go anyplace.

"He uses the Taser on me if I don't do what he wants. Like he got mad because I kept looking him in the eye. So he shocked me." She twisted back and forth in the swivel chair. "And when I didn't want to call him Sir, he fixed that in a hurry."

I hated to keep asking. I knew how cruel it was. But I had to know. "That's not really what I meant," I said carefully.

Jenny stilled, and I saw that she finally understood. "Oh. No. Even though all the clothes he had in the closet for me were sexy ones. He hates the way my face looks. He was hoping I'd look better once the scars healed. Everything he read online said it might take as long as a year. But it's been ten months, and it's pretty clear I'm never going to look normal again." She regarded me with something I thought might be pity. "I figure that's why he took you. You must be the new me. Only with fewer defects."

Jenny and I did look alike, I realized. Blue eyes, pale skin, long dark hair.

An icy finger traced my spine as I stared at this ruined girl. "Forget that! I'm not waiting around to see what he wants me for. I'm getting out of here."

She shook her head. "You can't."

"Just because the front door is chained doesn't mean there's not a way out. It's not like this is a supermax prison. It's a motor home." Using my good hand, I awkwardly got to my feet, ignoring how it made my head hurt even worse. I pushed aside the brown polyester curtain that led to the driving end of the RV. The windshield and side windows were also covered with silver tarps. The faint light from behind me revealed a deep dash made of fake wood. The driver and passenger seats were shaped like recliners. Any flat surface was piled with stuff.

My pulse was a drum in my ears as I realized to my horror that neither the driver's nor the passenger's side had a door. The only way in or out was the door in the living area, the one that was chained shut. The one with Rex on the other side.

The windows operated on sliders. I pinched the bar on the driver's-side window, but it refused to move. Pressing my cheek against the cold glass, I saw that a piece of wood had been wedged into the outside track. On the passenger side, the window was the same.

It felt like my throat was closing. Like my heart was about to give out. I could hear my own breaths, shallow and fast.

I recognized this panicky feeling. The first time it happened, I was eight and we were living with this guy named Adam and his kid, Cameron, in Hebron, Nebraska. I'd been retrieving a Monopoly game from the top shelf of the living room closet when suddenly Cameron, who was a year older, closed the door. I heard him giggle as he stuck a dining room chair under the handle, the way people did in movies.

No matter how hard I turned the knob or slammed my shoulder against the door, it refused to budge. With the wood of the door on one side of me and the winter coats pressing against the other, I started feeling like I might smother. Or that my heart would explode. In less than five minutes, I went from shouting, kicking, and pounding to crying and hyperventilating. When Cameron let me out, he took one look at my face and burst into tears himself.

"Are you all right?" Jenny asked.

I didn't answer, just moved back into the living space.

I pounded one fist experimentally on the window. The blows sounded muffled. On the other side of the door, Rex growled. He seemed close, like his feet were on the top step.

Jenny winced. "There's nothing to break them with. It's not like he left a hammer or a crowbar in here."

Suddenly, I knew what Bruce Lee would do. "Maybe we could try this!" I said, moving until I found the right angle. Taking a deep breath, I leaned my upper body to one side while I brought my left knee to my chest, so that I was standing on my right leg like a stork. As I said *this*, my left foot shot out and hit the window with as much force as I had ever kicked a heavy bag. But it didn't break. It didn't crack. It didn't even bend. I stumbled backward. Jenny reached out her hand and steadied me before I fell over.

The kick, which had taken every last bit of my energy, had accomplished so little that Rex didn't even start barking. He just growled louder.

"I think all the windows are made of plastic, not glass," Jenny said.

After Cameron had locked me in the closet, I couldn't stand elevators, small rooms, or crowded movie theaters. Even getting stuck in traffic was torture. Those other times were just a product of my imagination. But this RV was just as real as the closet had been. Only no one was coming to let me out.

Once my mom learned about my fight with Tim, she'd probably think I'd run away. Even if she didn't, no one would know to look for me here. Sir had snatched me from a deserted parking lot. Nobody would be able to connect the dots from me to this place.

Jenny had been here for months. That meant we could be here until we were both officially adults.

Until we were old.

Until Sir died.

And then we did, too.

JENNY DOWD

LISTENING TO REX'S GROWL WAS NEARLY UNBEARABLE. BUT HE was safely behind a locked door, while Savannah was in here with me, breathing so fast it was almost a pant, clearly freaking out.

"Are you okay?" I asked her. Savannah was starting to remind me of a broken doll.

Her voice was so soft I couldn't tell if she was talking to me or herself. "I can't be here forever and ever. Stuck in this tiny space." She looked toward the door, and her voice got stronger. "When's he coming back?"

I shrugged one shoulder. "Maybe today, maybe tomorrow. He wants to put a cast on your arm, but the swelling has to go down before he can do that. He said that might take a couple of days."

She bit her lower lip. It was flawless, red and plump. "And how long was I out?"

"I think close to twenty-four hours. I don't have a clock or anything. The only way I can tell time is by looking at the sky through the vent in the hall."

"Then I'd better hurry and figure out how to get us out of here before he comes back."

With Savannah's plans and schemes and refusal to accept reality, she reminded me of me.

Me when I first came here. Me when I had made the split-second decision to try to escape the first day.

When Rex had leapt toward me, I had felt his hot breath wash across me. Smelled the stink of it, the fug of something rotting. When he clamped his jaws onto my face, I instinctively pulled back. It didn't even hurt. Not at first. The feeling was not so much of pain, but of pressure. Still, I knew I was in terrible trouble. Knew Rex was doing damage. And that if he managed to knock me off my feet, he would surely kill me.

Sir was yelling, "*Nein! Aus! Aus!*" Finally, he pressed the Taser against Rex, holding the trigger to deliver a sustained shock. The dog's jaws instantly loosened. I heard him squealing as he thrashed in the dirt.

Meanwhile, despite my bound wrists, I somehow managed to push myself to my feet. With my hands holding my face together, I was able to stagger forward a single step. Then another. My hands were coated with blood, but I still made for the gap.

Then Sir grabbed me.

The months since had been a slow-motion nightmare. After they were stitched, the wounds swelled and turned red, inflamed from infection. Fever left me weak and delirious. I slept for days on end. But even in the depths of it, whenever I was alone and aware, I left fingerprints everywhere. In case one day, after I was gone, the police thought to search the motor home.

Sir eventually brought me a bottle of antibiotics with a missing label. Had he lied to a doctor? Bought them from someone on the street? Slowly, my body recovered, even if my face remained a horror. At first, Sir tried to make me be the obedient girl of his twisted dreams, grooming me for the day my scars would finally heal. Now he left me alone for two or three days at a time.

Whenever he did come by with more food or toilet paper, I tried to stay out of sight. But even in the bedroom I could hear him muttering and swearing. About how I was no good to him now. Not with my disgusting scars.

So while Rex had nearly killed me, he'd also saved me. But if I went back out there, if I tried again to escape, Rex would definitely finish the job. And I thought Sir would let him.

Now I grabbed Savannah's chin, her perfect unmarred chin, and forced her to turn toward me. "Look at me! This is what happens when you try to get out. It's a miracle I didn't die out there. Sometimes I wish I had."

With a twist of her shoulder and a press of her arm, Savannah easily broke my grip and stepped away. Like kicking the window, it seemed something she might have learned from that Bruce Lee book of hers.

Her gaze suddenly sharpened. I turned my head to see what she was looking at.

She pointed. "What about the vent?" Made of

translucent plastic, it was in the hallway ceiling, next to the bathroom, and could be raised a few inches with a metal arm. On warm days, I kept it open.

We moved to stand directly under it. I felt the floor dip under my weight. I was standing on the spongy part, the spot that got wet every time it rained hard enough and the vent leaked. The vent was held in place with six screws: one on each corner and then two in the middle, where there was a dividing arm.

"But I don't have a screwdriver."

I'd searched the motor home from top to bottom, but I'd found nothing I could use against Sir.

And nothing I could use against myself.

> *The control of our being is not unlike the combination of a safe. One turn of the knob rarely unlocks the safe; each advance and retreat is a step toward one's final achievement.*
>
> —BRUCE LEE

SAVANNAH TAYLOR

TERRIBLE THINGS HAD HAPPENED TO JENNY, BUT THERE WAS no time to pity her. I had to focus on getting out before he came back. Still, I tried to sound patient. "Come on, there must be something we could use to get it off. It's only six screws."

"Even if we were able to get the vent off, and somehow managed to climb out, we'd just be up on top of this thing." Jenny pointed at the ceiling. "On top of a slippery plastic roof twelve feet above the ground with nothing to cushion us once we jumped—or fell—off. And even if we managed to get down without breaking an ankle, there's Rex." She put her hands to her scarred face. Her eyes peeped at me through the cracks between her fingers.

"I know you're scared of the dog." I also knew that was an understatement.

Her voice shook. "He's been specially trained to kill people."

Remembering the dog's long, sharp teeth as he lunged at me through the door gap, I could believe it. Still I found the flaw in her argument. "If Rex is trained to kill people, then why hasn't he killed that guy? Killed Sir?"

"Because he's the one who trained him, only in some kind of foreign language like Dutch or German. But even if Rex didn't kill us, he'd start barking and then Sir would catch us. And he's got that Taser and the big knife on his belt." She shivered, her fingertips tracing the red ridges of her face.

"It's different now, Jenny. There's two of us. With two of us, we have a real chance." My words were as much for myself as they were for her. "A chance to get past the dog. A chance to escape even if Sir hears us. Besides, no matter what happens, we're going to have to deal with him. Inside or out there. Whatever he's planning for either of us can't be good."

I was so tired. My whole body ached, and my head felt like there was something inside that wanted out. Pressing the heels of my hands against my temples, I ignored the little voice that suggested I needed to lie down again.

"We can't go out there." Jenny shook her head, her face stubborn and set. "We'd die."

I took a deep breath and made myself say the truth. "Face it, Jenny. All our choices probably end in death. It might just come down to how fast it is. And maybe faster would be better." I couldn't force Jenny to come with me. So I would have to leave her behind while I tried to go for help.

"If you won't go with me, at least help me get out so I can try. It's better if I leave while it's still dark. While Sir's asleep and maybe the dog is, too."

"Will you even fit?"

Ignoring how the room started to spin, I tipped my head back to measure the space with my eyes. The vent was a little more than a foot square. "I think I will if I put my hips on the diagonal." I would do it even if I had to strip naked. Even if it left gouges in my flesh. When I dropped my gaze back to Jenny, a wave of dizziness rolled over me. With my good hand, I steadied myself on the wall.

Her dark eyebrows drew together. "Are you okay?"

"I'm fine," I lied. Everything hurt, and I was so tired. I forced myself to ask the question that had been circling in my thoughts like a shark. "Have there been other girls?"

"I don't think so. And you're the first person I've seen except Sir in the last ten months."

I guessed that counted as good news. If we were the first two girls to get taken, then Sir hadn't had a chance to get good at it.

I flipped the switch in the bathroom to get more light, then stood on tiptoe for a closer look at the screws.

The top of each one was marked with two grooves in the shape of a cross. "They're uh"—I tried to remember the term—"Phillips head screws. And you're sure you don't have a screwdriver?"

She rolled her eyes. "Do you really think he'd let me have something I could stab him with?"

Sarcastic Jenny was better than freaked-out Jenny. "I'm assuming that means you also don't have a table knife."

What else might fit in the groove? "Do you have a dime? Or wait—maybe I have one in my wallet."

"I don't have one, and neither do you." Seeing my confusion, Jenny elaborated. "I looked in your wallet to figure out who you were, remember? All you have is two quarters and a nickel."

It was weird to think about how she had gone through my things while I was unconscious. Maybe living like a caterpillar in a jar for the past ten months had made her forget the concept of privacy.

After retrieving my wallet, I still attempted to use the coins I had, but they didn't fit in the slot. Next I tried to fit my library card into the cross. But the long straight edge was a tiny bit too wide, as was my Wilson ID card. My driver's license fit but was too flimsy. When I tried to turn it, it just flexed.

Then my eyes fell on the CDs next to the boom box. "Maybe one of these would work." With my good hand, I managed to open a CD case for a band I had never heard of. Four guys all with ridiculously overgrown beards.

She looked stricken. "But those are the only CDs I have."

Jenny was really starting to get on my nerves. "If this works, I'll buy you a million CDs. Besides, you'll still have the tapes." To demonstrate, I pressed the button for the boom box's tape player. Instead of playing some greatest hit from 1985, what came out was a girl's voice, high and pure, unaccompanied. The girl was singing about how she was going to fly away on a bright morning when life was over.

I pushed the button again to turn it off. I knew that voice. "Is that you?" I asked.

She looked away from me. "I'm in choir. Or at least I used to be. I record myself and then I play the song back and sing the harmony." Her face colored, flushing the parts that weren't already red. "It makes me feel less alone."

JENNY DOWD

SAVANNAH STOOD DIRECTLY UNDER THE VENT, HER HEAD TILTED back and her good arm straight overhead. "Righty-tighty, lefty-loosey," she chanted as she slowly turned the CD she'd finally managed to fit into one of the screws.

"What are you saying?" I asked.

Her eyes didn't shift from the point where the CD met the screw. "It's how you know which direction to turn."

"Isn't that just counterclockwise?"

She made a raspberry sound. "That's kind of hard to figure out, especially when it's over your head and not right in front of you." As she spoke, the CD slipped out of the screw slot. She squinted, poked her tongue out of the corner of her mouth, and reset the CD. Slowly, she began to twist the disc.

Savannah was so focused, without a single doubt. She

seemed to think that getting out was going to be easy. Like we could just unscrew the vent, pull it down, climb out, and go. Like there weren't worse things waiting for us out in the dark.

But what if she was right? What if it had been possible to leave all along, and I'd just been stupid enough to accept it this whole time?

A crow of triumph interrupted my thoughts.

"Yes!" After setting aside the CD, Savannah used her fingers to finish twisting out the newly loosened screw. She set it on the bathroom counter. Then with a grimace, she shook out her arm.

Rex was still out there. But Sir was probably asleep, the way Savannah said. And maybe she was even right that together we could figure out a way to get past the dog. After all, my wrists wouldn't be duct taped. And if I went with her, there would be two of us.

We could still fail. We could still be killed. But her question kept echoing through me. Which was worse? To die or to keep living like this?

For the past ten months, I'd been existing in a stupor. Hunkered down, telling myself that the most important thing was simply to survive. Savannah was forcing me to wake up.

She picked the CD up again and set the edge of the disc in the next screw, but this time when she turned, it didn't budge. She kept twisting it even as the silver plastic flexed and started to bend. Finally it broke. The snapping sound made us both jump. The broken piece fell to the carpet as she turned the CD to an unbroken edge. Now it lacked its earlier rigidity. Each time she tried to twist the screw, it was the disc that gave instead, creating a series of small cracks until finally a second big piece broke off. Meanwhile, the screw didn't seem to be moving at all.

"Maybe try a different screw?" I ventured.

Without saying anything, Savannah moved on to another screw. Eventually she was able to loosen it. But her victory came at the expense of all my CDs. She piled the increasingly smaller shards next to the bathroom sink.

When Savannah turned to set the second screw next to the first, she staggered and nearly lost her balance.

"Here. Let me do it." I held out my hand for the biggest remnant of CD. "You're so tired you can't even stand up. You should lie down for a while."

"I'm fine." Her face was covered by a slight sheen of sweat.

"You don't look fine." Savannah was starting to remind me of toddlers I babysat. The more tired they got, the more they protested they were wide awake. My gaze fell on her splinted arm. Her fingers looked like sausages, red and plump. "Look at your hand. It's all swollen."

"Yeah, well I think we have more important things to worry about than my hand." She made a face, but still handed over the CD shard. "Okay, okay, I'll sit down for a second." She leaned against the wall and slid down until her face was even with her knees. She tipped her head forward.

It took me a long time to seat the piece of CD in the screw. Thoughts crowded my head. If I let Savannah go out there by herself, how would she manage against Rex with one hand? And meanwhile, I would be all alone. Could I stand to go back to never having anyone to talk to? And it wasn't like staying put would keep me safe. Sir was already mad at me for things I couldn't control, like my face not healing. How much angrier would he be once he realized I had known what Savannah was doing and done nothing to stop it?

The piece of CD kept slipping out whenever I tried to turn it. My shoulder burned, and the pain began to crawl up the side of my neck. Finally I found the point where I generated enough force to keep the shard in the slot and turn. A spark of happiness traced through me as I twisted the plastic. And then it snapped into two pieces, neither of them bigger than an inch across.

The sound roused Savannah. She swore. "There has to be something else we can use." She awkwardly pushed herself to her feet. In the kitchen area, she rattled the cupboard door. "Why won't this open?"

"There's a latch. I guess you wouldn't want all your glasses falling out every time the RV took a turn." My fingers reached past her and pressed down on the plastic hook so that the door swung open. "Are you hungry?"

She swallowed hard at the sight of my food: SpaghettiOs, canned tuna and peaches, generic Wheat Thins, and a jar of peanut butter, as well as a glass and a plastic plate. "No," she said shortly.

"You should be," I said. "I ate while you were sleeping, but it's been at least twenty-four hours since you did."

With her good hand, she waved away the suggestion. "Please stop talking about food."

She managed to unlatch the single drawer tucked under the counter by herself. It was filled with a jumble of junk, including two metal spoons and a spork. She tried the corners of the spoon handles in a screw slot, but they were too big. After putting them back, Savannah looked at me with bleary eyes. "How much longer do we have until the sun comes up?"

In the hallway, I squinted up at the dark sky. Was it getting lighter? "I don't know. But it does seem like it's been a long time since it got dark."

Aimlessly, I pawed through the junk drawer. And then I saw it, wedged in the back corner. The metal potato peeler. It barely worked, taking big chunks of apple or potato along with the skin. But what about the rounded tip that was meant to dig out bruises? Could it also dig us out of here?

Ignoring the ache in my shoulder from holding my hand above my head for so long, I set it in another screw. The peeler was so flimsy that it bent in my grip as I twisted it. But eventually it loosened the third screw. Long minutes later, the fourth was free. I was starting to think that it all might actually work. There were only two more screws. If we could just climb out before Sir noticed and then find a weapon before Rex found us, maybe we would stand a chance.

But when I started on the remaining screws, they refused to budge. I pushed the peeler so hard that it broke, cutting the tips of my index and middle fingers. Pressing them against the palm of my other hand to stop the bleeding, I looked down at Savannah, curled up on the stained carpet, to see what she thought we should do now. The sound of her breathing, soft and regular, made me realize that she was asleep. I crouched to wake her. But what was the point? The screws weren't budging. I found myself lying down next to her.

I don't know how many hours went by. When I woke up, Savannah was swearing as she looked at the two remaining screws. "They're both stripped!"

I got to my feet and looked at the vent, squinting. I realized it was easier to see the screws because the sun had risen. Both screws were no longer topped with crosses. Now they were more like circles.

"But there are only two left."

Tears sparkled in her eyes. "It doesn't matter if there are two or twenty. There aren't edges to work against anymore."

And then things went from bad to worse. Outside, Rex began to bark.

After dropping to the floor, I scurried to the door. I pressed my eye to the tiny sliver where the tarp had slipped across the window. Through it, I saw Sir. A lightning bolt of fear shot down my spine. He was coming back.

"Get back into bed," I scream-whispered at Savannah, who was staring at me with blurry eyes. "Get back into bed and pretend you're still unconscious."

AMY DOWD

WHEN I GOT THE PHONE CALL ABOUT SAVANNAH TAYLOR, THE missing girl, I hadn't thought about my Jenny for almost ninety minutes. Which was nearly a record.

Especially on a Saturday. On weekdays at the bank, I could lose myself in the minutiae of the day. Talk to customers about the houses and cars they were buying, nod along as they enumerated the merits of wrap-around porches and side-curtain air bags.

In my desk drawer was a photo of a four-year-old Jenny. She had her arms wrapped tight around my neck and her head tucked into my shoulder. Looking at that photo hurt. Physically hurt. It set off a hollow ache in my chest and stomach, even my arms and legs.

But that wasn't the reason I had hidden it away. No, I had done it so that no one would ask about her. I'd also changed my nameplate and business cards to my maiden name, even though the divorce wasn't finished yet. I couldn't deal with the way people looked at me when they saw the name Dowd.

The pain was no longer fresh and raw. Now it was like a throb, as constant as the hidden beat of my heart.

I always hoped that Jenny would come to me in a dream. But she never did. Bob said she had for him. Why not me? Was she mad that I had accepted her death?

Over the past ten months, I'd gained twenty pounds. Eating mindlessly helped my brain go quiet, as I rhythmically chewed and swallowed until the bag or box or bowl was empty. And there was no point in working out, in running on a treadmill to nowhere.

No matter how I spent my time, I was always one minute farther away from Jenny. And the space between us just kept getting wider.

It wasn't like she had fallen through the cracks. Night after night, her disappearance was the lead story on the local news and then the national news. A pretty white teen from an intact family? The media ate that up.

The cops used dogs, helicopters, psychologists, hypnotists, and even a psychic who offered her services for free. They searched creeks and abandoned buildings. Questioned known child molesters. Staked out Island Tan at the exact time and day Jenny had disappeared, questioning anyone who might have heard or seen something.

Only they turned up nothing.

They lifted hundreds of fingerprints from the tanning shop and, one by one, ran them through the system.

A few turned out to belong to people with criminal records, mostly girls who had shoplifted. A sizable percentage belonged to unknown people.

It was like Jenny had been teleported into a different dimension. I still lay awake at night trying out different scenarios. Had the dad or boyfriend of a client taken sick notice of her? Or was it someone she knew well? Had someone robbed the place and then decided to take the only witness as well? Was it even possible that she had left, run off with the money from the register? But her phone never pinged, and how far could you get on a couple of hundred dollars?

At work, I sometimes let myself pretend that she was at school. On weekends, I might imagine for a few hours that she was at a friend's house. My counselor called these thoughts "defensive delusions."

Pretending was the only way I could summon the energy to draw up contracts or make a simple meal, but there were times the mental game was so easy it scared me.

"Is it normal?" I'd asked the counselor at our last appointment. "Is this something other people do?"

"There is no normal," she had said. "There are only things that allow you to survive."

Did Bob still go to counseling? Blake had gone a half dozen times and then refused to go anymore.

The day Jenny went missing was the day our family shattered. As the hours stretched into days and then weeks, I shut down. Bob accused me of being cold. Of the two of us, I'd always been the realist. Certainly, I'd have liked to imagine that Jenny had fallen and hit her head and forgotten who she was. Or that she'd been forced to steal the money or perhaps been trafficked and now was too embarrassed to come home. But of course those things weren't true, so I'd had to accept that our daughter was dead. I wanted to believe that it happened quickly and she hadn't suffered.

But that was probably as much a fantasy as Bob's belief that she was alive and we just needed to find her.

After Jenny went missing, Blake started spending all his time at his friends' houses. At first because their parents could give him the things we couldn't—regular meals, a schedule, adults who weren't shouting or weeping. But when we tried to resume our lives, Blake still chose to be with his friends as much as possible. I remember surfacing once to think how strange it was that we had become like distant relatives to our own son, trying to maintain contact with phone calls and regular visits.

While Blake found replacement families, I didn't want to keep pretending that we were a real family anymore. It was just too painful. Except that once Bob moved out, I didn't feel any better. I had craved silence, but it turned out that being alone in a quiet, empty house was worse.

The only pleasure I could look forward to was taking a small purple sleeping pill every night. Once I had emptied all those tiny pills into my palm. If my daughter was dead, I wanted to be dead, too. Something made me pour them back into the bottle.

I didn't even feel human anymore. Most of the other humans I interacted with seemed as stupid as lambs being raised for slaughter. Not realizing their days were pointless and would soon end.

The only ones who could reach me were those parents who had survived the death of a child. For a few minutes, I could respect their pain. But even then, I found it didn't last. Yes, your five-year-old might have died from cancer, but at least you'd been there for those last moments. At least you knew what happened. Yes, you might have lost your twelve-year-old to a drunk driver, but now you'd be able to go through all those stages of grieving: denial, anger, whatever.

I was stuck.

That's why when I heard about In Trevor's Memory, I knew I had to volunteer. All the volunteers had one thing in common: missing children. Some eventually found. Many not.

For another mother or father, I could be the person I had needed when Jenny was taken from us.

And now I would be that person for Lorraine Taylor.

SIR

REX KNEW ENOUGH NOT TO TRY TO FOLLOW ME INTO THE RV, but his front paws were on the top step. "*Raus!*" I ordered him. Out! He backed off, his desire battling with his fear.

I understood how he felt.

After closing the door, I set down the supplies I had bought at Michaels crafts, including a pair of cheap white satin gloves. I would cut the fingers off one and then slide it up her arm. Then I would dip the plaster-of-paris bandages in water and wrap them around the glove.

I came to a halt in the bedroom doorway. Even though more than thirty-six hours had passed, the two girls were nearly just as I had left them. The new girl lay on her back under the covers. Jenny was curled on top of the comforter, facing her.

And they were both absolutely still. Unmoving.

My breath caught in my chest. Could they be dead?

A jolt ran from my head to my heels. But it was followed by something unexpected.

Relief. I didn't have to figure out what to do about Jenny, with her ruined face. I didn't have to decide if I wanted a second broken girl.

My shoulders loosened. I took a deep breath of the RV's stale air.

And then Jenny's eyelids fluttered open. I turned on the light.

"How's my patient?" I asked.

"She's still asleep." Jenny rubbed her eyes and sat up.

The new girl didn't even twitch. I squeezed between the bed and the wall and sat next to her. Her splint rested on top of the comforter. Her fingers were swollen and red. Not at all the condition I had hoped to find them in. Casting her wrist would have to wait.

She lay flat on the pillow, her eyes closed. The left side of her face was scabbed. It looked bad, but of course Jenny's face was much worse. And it would never get any better.

The undamaged side was pale, but her cheek was flushed. Now that I was close, I could hear her fast and shallow breathing. Could she have an infection even though the broken bone hadn't pierced the skin? Or maybe she had picked up some kind of germ when her face scraped along the roadway.

When I laid a hand on her forehead, her skin was cool. But it was also damp, clammy with sweat. A wave of disgust rolled over me. I jerked my hand back and then wiped it on my coveralls.

I looked at Jenny. "Has she been like this the whole time?"

"Savannah? Pretty much."

I tilted my head. "How do you know her name?"

Jenny's gaze darted to the other girl's face. "Um, I looked in her wallet."

I glanced back at Savannah. Her eyes were still closed. But for some reason, I felt like she and Jenny had just exchanged a look.

Maybe it had been a mistake, putting them together. I could pick this girl up and carry her out the door right now. Walk a hundred feet, and put her in the other RV I had hauled here a month ago. I had already set it up with clothes and kitchen supplies and everything she might need. All of it bought cash-only at the Salem Goodwill, over an hour away. I hadn't wanted to risk running into someone who knew me. Someone who would wonder why I was buying clothes for a teenage girl when I didn't have children. When, as far as they knew, I didn't even have a girlfriend. The whole time I had worn a baseball cap pulled low over my eyes, in case the store had security cameras.

It had been exciting getting everything ready for her. It had been like it was a year ago, when I'd been preparing for Jenny. I still remembered the night I had first spotted her. She was locking up the door of Island Tan late at night, everything dark around her except the light over her beautiful face. I had spent a few weeks figuring out her schedule, finding the best time to take her.

And then Jenny had gone and ruined everything.

Sure, she was compliant. She called me Sir, the way

I taught her to. She followed all the rules. She trembled every time I entered the RV. All of those were good things.

But I couldn't get past how her face looked now, despite my best efforts. Even if I closed my eyes, how could I want to kiss torn lips, to hear the ragged breathing through her gashed nostril?

"When she wakes up," I reminded Jenny, "don't forget to teach her the rules."

Jenny nodded her head like a bobble doll. "Yes, Sir."

I had thought Jenny could help me make Savannah the kind of girl I had dreamed of for so long. Pretty. Compliant. And afraid.

But now I wondered. Had I made the same mistake twice?

And was it too late to fix it?

The successful warrior is the average man
with laser-like focus.

—BRUCE LEE

SAVANNAH TAYLOR

"IT'S NOT TIM," I WHISPERED ONCE I WAS SURE SIR WAS REALLY gone. It also wasn't Mr. Fryer or Mr. Tae Kwan Do. I had been so anxious that the bottom of my feet and the backs of my knees were still sweating.

"If you know that, then you must have opened your eyes!" Jenny hissed. "What if he'd caught you? He was looking awfully suspicious." Her ruined mouth twisted. "And like he was making some kind of plan."

"I just peeped at him through my lashes. And you must have looked at him too," I countered.

"Normally all his attention is focused on me." Jenny crawled backward to the end of the bed and then got to her feet. "I could only risk it because he was looking at you."

"See, that's what I've been trying to tell you. The two of us can do things that one person could never manage by herself." I was still thinking about Sir. "I don't recognize him, but my mom's boyfriend has made us come with him to wrecking yards a couple of times while he looks for parts for his classic car. We must be at one of them. But I never really looked at the workers there."

"He told me that he saw me outside Island Tan and knew that I was meant for him," Jenny said. "Although I think he's changed his mind about that." She shivered. "I was so afraid he'd notice the screws were gone. Or even decide to check the trash." As I had scrambled under the covers, she had swept the screws and improvised tools into the bathroom garbage can.

How were we going to escape? We couldn't get out through the vent. The windows were made of something that refused to break. And the door had a chain padlocked across it.

Except whenever he came inside, he had to unlock it. "Next time he comes back, we're going to have to hurt him," I said with more courage than I felt. Sir's words, his tone of voice, and the brief glimpse I'd had of him had helped me understand why Jenny was so afraid of him. "We just need to disable him long enough for us to get away."

Jenny was already shaking her head. "If we try anything, he'll just hurt us."

"Not if we gang up on him the second he starts to come inside."

Ignoring how my head and body ached, I started to search the RV again, but now I was looking for a weapon. The table and bench were built in the wall. The two swivel chairs were bolted down, as was the couch. No freestanding

lamps, just lights in the ceiling. I could try swinging the
boom box at his head, but it was made of plastic, and the
cord of the attached mic looked too short to try to wrap
around his neck.

When I pressed the tines of a spork from the junk
drawer against my skin, they barely made a dent. The end
of the potato peeler had been dulled by our assault on the
vent.

Could I combine things to make a weapon? Maybe I
could embed the lid of a can in a wooden broom handle.
As I imagined the sharp metal edge slicing his face, I felt
both horrified and exhilarated. "Do you have a broom or a
mop or anything like that?"

"No. Just one of those hand vacuums. It's under the
sink." Not following my thoughts, Jenny added, "I try, but
it's hard to keep this place clean."

Clean gave me another idea. "Do you have any spray
cleaner?"

"Dish soap?" she offered.

So much for blinding him with chemicals. What would
Bruce Lee do? He was famous for his skill with nunchucks,
two pieces of wood connected by a short chain. In movies,
he could fight off a whole room full of people, swinging
one end through the air to hit his attackers in the head or
crotch. I didn't have any wooden sticks or a chain, but . . . I
checked the cupboard again. "Do you have a pair of tights?"

"Yeah." Without asking why, Jenny went into the bedroom and returned with a pair of black fishnet stockings.
The sight of them made me shiver as I thought of Sir buying them for her. Clenching the waistband with my teeth,

with my good hand, I slipped the can of SpaghettiOs inside one leg and then shook it until it fell all the way to the toe. Grabbing the top of the leg, I raised my hand, the dangling can swinging back and forth. "Step back," I told Jenny. Then I spun the improvised nunchuck around my head and snapped it down. The can thumped so hard on the couch cushion that it left a dent.

Jenny and I exchanged a grin. "Next time he comes in the door, I'll hit him in the head with that. If he doesn't get knocked out right away, I'll keep hitting. You grab the Taser. When we leave, we'll padlock the door behind us so he can't follow."

The smile fell from her face. "But what will we do about Rex?"

"We can use the Taser on him like Sir did when you were getting bitten."

"But what if you miss when you swing the can? Or it doesn't hurt Sir enough?" She was trembling. "You don't want to make him mad."

I made a sound like a laugh. "I think it's too late for that."

"But you know kung fu." Her voice shook. "I don't know anything."

"That's something we can fix," I said.

"What is" is more important than "what should be."

—BRUCE LEE

SAVANNAH TAYLOR

"THE BASICS OF SELF-DEFENSE ARE ACTUALLY PRETTY EASY." I tried to project confidence. I thought I knew them well enough to teach them—but could Jenny learn? If I had learned anything about martial arts, it was that more than half of it was attitude. If you believed you couldn't do something, then you couldn't. But the reverse was also true.

Jenny squared her shoulders. "Then show me."

I let go of the makeshift nunchuck. The can thumped on the couch. "The first step is to protect your head. Always keep your hands up in front of your face." I demonstrated, but only with my good arm, which felt really strange.

Jenny raised her hands, which she had curled into fists. But her thumb was tucked inside her fingers.

I shook my head. "Don't even worry about making fists,"

I said. "If you make one with your thumb inside like that, and then hit him, you might break it. Just keep your hands open and up. If he tries to grab or punch you, raise your arm just enough to block it with the side of your wrist." I raised my right hand, parrying an imaginary blow while still keeping my forearm at a right angle. "Now try to hit me on the right side of my head."

Jenny pulled her hand back for a slap. I raised my forearm a few inches and blocked it. Our wrists clashed.

"Ouch!" She rubbed her wrist. "That hurts."

"My sifu has this saying—" I started, but Jenny interrupted.

"Sifu?"

"*Sifu* means 'teacher.' My sifu says you should put hard bones in soft places. Now you try. Put your hands up and block me." She did and easily blocked my slap, then a right roundhouse I threw.

Although I knew her wrist must still be hurting from the clash of our bones, now she wasn't even wincing. I'd been expecting her to have the slightly stunned look most women did when they realized that martial arts was going to involve physical contact and even some actual pain. But Jenny, with her scars, her knowledge of teeth and Tasers, was more familiar with pain than I was.

She was far stronger than she looked.

Feeling more confident in her abilities, I continued. "A punch is basically like a fast push. Strike with the heel of your hand. Remember, hard bones, soft places. So you've got the eyes, the nose"—with my good hand I demonstrated lightly on myself—"and the neck. And if you catch him under the chin and push, he'll have to go where you push."

I ducked into the bedroom and came back with the pillow. Holding the back of the pillow in the center, I lifted it to head height, off to one side. "Pretend this is his face."

She grunted as she threw her first strike, hard enough that I staggered. "Nice!" I adjusted my stance so my shoulder could swing away to better absorb the impact. "Don't pull your arm back before you hit him, or he'll know what you're doing." I thought of Daniel but pushed the thought away. I had to focus. "Always keep your elbows in front of your ribs. Now hit some more." As she struck again and again, I grunted each time. "That's right. Pivot from the feet. Use your hips."

My shoulder aching, I finally dropped the pillow. "That's very good. You move well. A lot of people don't realize that the power of your hands comes from your feet and hips."

Jenny ducked her head, but I thought she looked proud. "I ran track in middle school."

"That should really help your kicks. A good place to aim for is the groin. Think of making contact with your shoelaces."

She kicked in the air with her toe pointed. "Like a scoop?"

I nodded. "Exactly. Exactly like that! Or kick him in the knee with the bottom or side of your shoe. With his knee dislocated, he couldn't chase after us. Kicks are good for keeping distance. But if he gets in too close, raise your knee just like you're climbing the stairs and hit him in the groin. If you lean back, you'll give it more force." Since I didn't have two hands to hold the pillow, I had Jenny practice both kicks and knee strikes in the air.

"Even if you end up on the ground, you can still kick him. Smash his knees, his groin, even his ankles." I thought back to what Sifu had said. Was it just two days ago? "The main rule is that there are no rules. Do whatever you have to do. Scratch or bite or gouge his eyes."

Outside, Rex started to bark again.

Jenny clutched my arm. "He's already coming back!"

We weren't nearly ready. Should I position myself on the far side of the door, where he wouldn't see me at first? Or on the near side where I could strike as soon as possible? What if I tried to hit him with the can just as Jenny was striking him and I ended up hurting her?

I chose the near side, swinging the can over my shoulder. It thumped painfully on my lower back. Jenny stood opposite me, her hands near her face, her open palms ready to strike him or grab the Taser.

Sourness spread over the back of my tongue. My pulse slammed in my ears.

And we waited for the door to open.

DANIEL DIAZ

YESTERDAY IN THE SCHOOL OFFICE, ANOTHER STUDENT HAD overheard Savannah's mom telling my dad about her disappearance. By the time the last bell rang, everyone was talking about Savannah, even people I was sure had no idea who she was. I started asking around, hoping to uncover new information. Maybe someone else at school knew her better, was in touch with her, or was giving her a place to crash. Maybe I could pass on the info to my dad, put his and her mom's minds to rest.

But no one really knew anything, except Nevaeh. She lived two doors down from the house Savannah shared with her mom and Tim. Nevaeh said that more than once she'd heard an angry man yelling inside the house. Just a man shouting. No one yelling back.

Since Savannah's home life was bad, it made sense that

she had taken off. It even explained why she had lied to me. Someone else must have been in the upper lot, someone she had arranged to wait for her. But there were other possible explanations. Darker ones. Tim could have been lying in wait. And it even turned out that, over the last few months, a couple of girls had thought a slow-moving car was tailing them for a few blocks. One I'd heard about before, the other was news to me.

Last night, I'd lain awake until four in the morning, replaying my last conversation with Savannah, looking for clues.

This morning, I biked back to our dojo and locked my bike to a street sign. On foot, I started where I had last seen Savannah Thursday night. On the concrete steps that led up to the upper parking lot.

It had been less than forty hours since she had turned to look back at me from these very steps.

Then she had gotten to the top, turned the corner, and gone—where? And why would she have gone someplace without her phone? She had definitely lied about her mom waiting for her. Did she have a friend outside of school? Or even a secret boyfriend? But if she did, why had it felt like she'd almost said yes to the idea of going to the winter formal with me?

Nevaeh had given me Savannah's home address. My plan was to retrace Savannah's steps, or at least my best guess of what they would have been, and look for clues. And once I got to her house, what then? I remembered how some dark emotion had flickered over her face when she talked about Tim. It was somehow worse that he wasn't even her official stepdad, just her mom's boyfriend. According to my dad, he had already admitted to Savannah's mom that he had argued with her. Could he have hurt her? At the thought, my hands balled into fists.

What would I do if I saw him coming out of the house? Or what about simply knocking on the door and demanding answers? My dad would get mad if I confronted Tim. But I wasn't sure I could leave him alone.

At the top of the steps, I turned and looked back. The corner of the building blocked me from seeing the spot where I had been Thursday night. Which meant that even if I had hung around, I wouldn't have been able to see what happened to Savannah once she reached the top. But I hadn't been looking, had I? I had believed her when she said her mom was giving her a ride home.

And if she had lied about that, maybe she had lied about other things, the way Dad had implied.

Lost in thought, I cut through the parking lot.

But something nagged at me. Something out of place. Finally, I stopped, turned, and scanned the lot, which held a half dozen cars.

Nothing jumped out at me. I was already turning back, already rehearsing what I would say to that jerk Tim if I saw him, when I spotted it.

A gray beanie, tangled low in the blackberry bushes at the back of the lot.

My stomach bottomed out. *No,* I thought. *No, please, God, I'm not seeing this.*

I walked over. With a shaking hand, I reached out and pulled the hat free from the brambles. Dark strands of hair clung to it. Long dark hair, just like Savannah's. In one spot, about a dozen hairs were clustered together.

As if they had been pulled out during a struggle.

In my mind's eye, I replayed standing outside with Savannah after class. The way she looked at me as she pulled on her hat.

This hat.

Something bad had happened here.

And I hadn't heard a thing.

SIR

CARRYING A WRENCH, I STARTED BACK TOWARD THE RV THAT held Jenny and Savannah.

I basically grew up with a wrench in my hand. Before I was born, my dad began this business on a stretch of land next to a country road. He'd been a shade tree mechanic who sometimes ended up with cars when his customers couldn't pay. He dismantled them and sold the parts, and over time, that became his main line of business. He bought cars that weren't worth fixing. At auctions, he bid on abandoned vehicles. Now there were acres of pasture covered with hundreds of cars and trucks. They lay in long, winding rows, many of them twisted and crumpled, as if made of paper and not steel. But they still contained so much that could be salvaged and sold. Head- and tail-lights, batteries, transmissions, radiators, catalytic converters. Engines. Rearview and sideview mirrors. Unbroken windshields if the car had been rear-ended. Bumpers if the car had been T-boned. My dad kept the high-demand parts in a cinderblock warehouse he built himself. The rest he pulled after a customer placed an order.

My dad was real friendly to customers, but not to us, his family. We knew his friendliness was just for show. A mask. To us, he was always Sir. That Sir set the tone. Kept us in line.

But we didn't appreciate it. My brother moved out his senior year of high school. (He's been dead for two years now. Cirrhosis of the liver.) My sister got married as soon as she graduated. And I joined the service when I was eighteen.

Back then, I thought my dad was the bad guy, the way he bossed us around. He didn't hesitate to whip off his belt at the first sign of back talk or even a certain look. Now I see that he just had high standards.

I spent over twenty years working stateside in the auto pool. Thanks to my dad, I could fix anything. I understood cars in a way I'd never understood people. I tried dating, but it never went the way I wanted. Every woman would ultimately reveal who she was. A whore. A feminazi. A yapper who wanted to tell me what she thought about things.

Two years ago, a lift failed and an engine block crushed my dad's chest. My mom said he had died the way he would have wanted to. And then she asked me to come home and run this place.

I left the service and stepped into my dad's boots. Literally. It was strange to realize that I was now the same size as him. And I found out that it was good to be your own boss. You could set your own hours. Make your own rules. And if people didn't like them, so what?

Just as she had with my dad, my mom took care of me. She

wasn't like women now, who didn't understand that a man was king of his castle. Women who wanted you to pay for dinner but didn't think they owed you anything afterward.

I checked out dating websites, but my mom was quick to figure out what was wrong with each potential date: hardened, trampy, mouthy, too old, raising another man's brats.

She said I needed someone like her. My dad had started dating her when he was in his twenties and she was still in middle school. He had shaped her into the woman she was. She didn't see that wasn't exactly possible nowadays, especially when you were forty-two.

But then last year, Mom died. She was not a complainer. By the time she finally went to the doctor, it was too late. The cancer was everywhere. She passed in the hospital less than two weeks after her diagnosis.

I missed her, of course. But she had also been a brake on me. I had started thinking about a way to get what I wanted. What I needed. What I deserved. But I hadn't been sure my mother would agree with my plans. Once she was gone, it was time to come into my own.

Driving a variety of cars I coaxed back to life, I started searching, keeping my eyes open for the right girl. The girl I had always dreamed of. Slender, pale skin, long dark hair, something vulnerable in her expression.

Once I found the right one, I planned to control everything about her. She would dress in the clothes I gave her. She would be demure and feminine. She would address me only as Sir, and she would never talk back.

I would create the perfect girl.

If Jenny had stayed pretty, maybe she could have been the one. Even so, I had learned a lot from her. It wasn't totally her fault that things had gone so wrong, but at the same time, you had to know when to cut your losses.

Then I spotted Savannah. I had first seen her when she came in with her mom and stepdad, dragged along while he picked up some parts for his 1968 Camaro. The whole time I had been talking to him, she had her face in her phone. Looking at her sulky expression, I thought how disrespectful she was being, not even bothering to hide her boredom.

She needed to be taught a lesson. And I was just the person to do it.

Since I had her address, it hadn't been hard to find her again. I followed her as she walked to her kung fu school, cutting away and then back a couple of times in case she turned around. But she never did.

That night I parked down the street and picked up my binoculars. Sitting in the darkness, I watched her through the floor-to-ceiling windows. Even though Savannah was the youngest in the class, she held her own.

I came back night after night, figuring out her schedule. Figuring out the best place to take her. I wanted a girl with a little more spunk than Jenny. A spark. Who wouldn't just hang her head and say yes sir, no sir. Someone who was more of a challenge. Taming Jenny had been like taming a dog. She was already hardwired to be loyal.

But this girl, this Savannah, she was a fighter. That was why I had picked her. But didn't they say the thing that drew you to someone would ultimately be the thing that pushed you away? Like if you were attracted to a person who was always the life of the party, by the time the relationship ended, you would be sick of their partying ways.

So I had picked a fighter, and that was exactly what I had gotten. Savannah had fought me in the parking lot. She had jumped out of the van when it was moving. And though she was injured now, as soon as she healed up, she would probably be plotting my demise.

This morning, looking down at her, wondering if she was really as unconscious as Jenny claimed, I realized that I'd made a huge mistake.

I just had to figure out how to fix it. Without making too much of a mess. Sewing up Jenny's face had been disgusting. Trying to kill two girls who did not want to die would surely be even more difficult and bloody.

Now as Rex barked and ran in circles around me, I crawled underneath the RV and found the white drain plug for the fresh water tank. It had no valve. It was easy to undo.

And then all the water poured out onto the ground. I didn't even mind when it soaked the knees of my pants. Sometimes you had to do things that you didn't want to. That were a little bit unpleasant. That might even seem, from an outsider's perspective, wrong.

In four or five days, the girls would be past causing anyone any trouble. Past doing anything at all.

And I already had the RV I had originally prepared for Savannah.

Just waiting for a new girl.

DANIEL DIAZ

"DIAZ," MY DAD BARKED, EVEN THOUGH WITH CALLER ID HE must have seen it was me. He hadn't answered the first time I called, just sent it to voice mail. So I'd hung up and called back.

"Hey, Dad, sorry to bother you." My hand was sweating so much that it was hard to hold my phone. My other hand still held Savannah's beanie.

"Daniel, remember, I have Shop with a Cop today." His faux-patient tone sounded like it came through gritted teeth. Shop with a Cop gave kids from underprivileged backgrounds gift cards and assigned them a cop buddy so they could Christmas shop for themselves and their families.

I'd never been Christmas shopping with my dad.

"I know, and I'm sorry," I said. "Only I'm at the dojo, and I just found Savannah's hat in the upper parking lot."

His tone changed. "Tell me more." After I explained, he said, "I'll be there in twenty."

Waiting in the parking lot, shivering in the chilly air, I felt hollowed out. The hat was proof that Savannah hadn't run away. That something bad must have happened to her here, with no one around to help her. With all the businesses closed and me pedaling away.

I kicked a pebble. When it landed, something black and round above it caught my eye. It was attached to the overhang sheltering the entrances of the four businesses that shared the lot.

A surveillance camera.

If I could see it, it could see me.

And if it could see me, had it seen Savannah?

I walked over. The camera was mounted directly over a dentist's office. The hours were listed on the door, including ten to one on Saturdays. Inside, a half dozen people were sitting in the waiting room. A mom and a boy of about ten were talking to a middle-aged woman in scrubs seated behind the reception desk.

I went inside and waited impatiently while the mom consulted her phone, rejecting date after date for a follow-up appointment for her kid. Finally they settled on one, and it was my turn.

"Checking in?" the woman asked. Her name tag read MACY. She clicked a key on her keyboard.

"Actually, I wanted to ask if that's your security camera outside?"

Macy's attention was still on her screen. "Yeah. We were having a problem with thefts. Drug addicts looking for painkillers, and then they'd steal anything that wasn't nailed down."

"I take classes at that kung fu school downstairs. A student went missing after class Thursday night. Her name's Savannah. I saw her go up those stairs, but she never made it home."

Macy's eyes flashed up to mine. A blue light started blinking on her desk, but she ignored it.

I raised Savannah's beanie. "This is her hat. I just found it caught in the blackberry bushes outside. I think something happened to her in your parking lot."

Before Macy could say anything, a man wearing scrubs and latex gloves appeared behind her.

"Macy! I need you back in room three to explain Mrs. Olsen's options to her." Without waiting for an answer, he turned on his heel.

"Yes, Dr. Yee," Macy said, getting up. She looked at me. "That camera just films the sidewalk in front of the door. Nothing else."

"Wait," I said as she started to leave. "Just tell me, does it run all the time?"

"Yes, but the memory only holds forty-eight hours' worth of video. After that, it records over it." She went down the hall.

Maybe Macy was hoping I would disappear while she was gone. Just like that footage would disappear tonight.

While I was waiting for her to return, my dad pulled up in his unmarked Ford Explorer. I went outside and told him what was going on.

"This is Savannah's hat." I held it out. "I saw her putting

it on right after class Thursday. So how did it end up in those bushes?" I pointed.

"How can you be sure it's hers?" He looked skeptical. "Everyone's got one of those."

"Maybe so, but this one has a clump of long, dark hair. Just like Savannah's. It looks like it was pulled out." Thinking about it made me feel like I'd gotten a side kick to the ribs.

Instead of directly taking the hat, Dad opened his trunk and got out a brown paper bag with EVIDENCE printed on the top in black block letters. He filled out the form on the front, then pouched it open and had me drop the hat inside.

After he put the bag in his trunk, we walked back into the dentist's office together. Before, I'd been practically invisible because I was a teenager. I still was invisible, but now it was because I was standing next to a man in a dark uniform with a badge on his chest, a Glock on one hip, and a Taser on the other. The waiting patients did not bother to hide their stares as they tried to figure out why he was there.

And my dad's presence changed everything for both Macy and Dr. Yee. After a brief whispered consultation, we were allowed into a small file room to view the video feed from the security camera. Well, initially my dad suggested that I head home while he watched it, but I refused, and he didn't argue.

But when Macy pulled up Thursday night's video on a computer monitor, I saw that she was right. It showed just the space directly in front of the door. Only the very edge of the frame captured a slice of the darkened parking lot. It didn't even reach as far back as the blackberry bushes.

After showing my dad how to move the video forward and backward, how to speed it up and slow it down, Macy left.

"Okay, what time did class end Thursday?" Dad asked.

"Seven thirty, and then Savannah and I mopped the floor. We probably left the dojo at seven forty-five."

"I'll start at seven thirty just to be sure." He set it to run at high speed, which meant that every ten seconds was collapsed into one. While it played, his finger hovered over the pause button, ready to hit it as soon as we saw something.

Only we didn't. The image never changed. A dark empty space. Not even a leaf or a piece of litter blew through.

As we watched and waited, I knew I had to bring up what I'd heard after I left his office. "I was asking around at school yesterday. Somebody said that earlier this week Courtney Schmitz thought a guy was driving real slow behind her on the way home from school. And about six weeks ago, Sara Ratliff was talking about something similar."

"What?" My dad hit the pause button and turned toward me. "And you didn't think to tell me until now? Don't you understand, Daniel? I am responsible for students' safety. And now you're saying that you were aware students were in danger and you did not inform me?" He wasn't raising his voice, but it still sounded like he was yelling.

"But I didn't really know, not until now. I only heard about Sara secondhand, and I didn't learn about what happened to Courtney until yesterday. And you know Sara. Courtney's just the same. They both like to be the center of attention, even if that means exaggerating things. I'd figured Sara was probably imagining it. Besides, the two cars weren't even the same."

"You're sitting there saying that when an actual girl has gone missing?" He made a frustrated growl. "That's not for you to say, Daniel. You let me be the judge of things like this. What about the driver? What did Courtney and Sara say he looked like?"

"I guess they said the windows were all steamed up so they couldn't see inside. About all they could tell was that the driver was a man."

Shaking his head, my dad turned away and pressed the button again. "If you'd told me back when it happened to Sara, we might have had a lead now. We might have had a name. But we've got nothing."

Was my dad right? Should I have run to him with second- or thirdhand information about Sara? "Even if some guys have been slowing down and looking at girls walking to school, creeping them out—I know that's not a crime." I threw my memory of past conversations back at him. "You're always talking about how you need to have something that will be prosecutable in a court of law."

He swore. "Well, now we've got nothing. Nothing about those cars, and nothing on this tape." I looked where he was—at the clock on the video: 8:30. A full forty-five minutes after Savannah should have come up the stairs.

Whatever had happened must have been out of reach of the camera. In the dark. No witnesses, not even a digital one.

Macy stuck her head in the door. "Any luck?"

143

"No." My dad turned back to the computer, ready to turn the video off.

And that was when we saw it.

Two feet entered the top corner of the frame. Savannah's. I didn't just recognize her shoes but the graceful way she moved.

Then behind her feet, two more appeared. Wearing what looked like work boots, although that was just a guess, because the lower legs were covered by dark coveralls. And suddenly the big feet were right behind Savannah's, so close the tips of his boots must have been hitting the heels of her worn Vans.

Savannah pivoted, broke away, and ran out of the frame. I gasped when she suddenly fell back into view, her body unnaturally stiff, toppling over like an axed tree.

"Taser," my dad muttered to himself.

For a moment, I saw Savannah's pale face as she landed hard, her head bouncing. Her hat was already gone. Then she went limp. A man's hands entered the frame and grabbed underneath her arms. And then they dragged Savannah away from the camera's view.

A few seconds later, a white van drove past the camera and out of the lot. It must have been parked in the far corner, where the security camera didn't reach. And I realized that Savannah had to be in the back of that van.

My dad slowed down the video, moving the footage back and forth, until he found the spot where the license plate was the most visible. Even then, the van was at an angle, so that only part of the plate showed, and it wasn't in focus.

My dad finally spoke. "Yesterday I interviewed Tim Hixon, Savannah's mother's boyfriend." He ran his tongue over his front teeth, his face scrunching up as if he were tasting something disgusting. "He's a mechanic. He dresses like that guy on this tape. Coveralls, boots."

"Where do think he took her?" My heart felt like it would beat out of my chest. "Do you think she's still alive?"

Dad took a flash drive from his pocket and slid it into the computer. "I'm going to go talk to Mr. Hixon and try to find out," he said as he copied the file. "I'd like to hear what he has to say about this."

JENNY DOWD

WHEN WE HAD HEARD SIR COMING BACK, SAVANNAH AND I froze, barely breathing, waiting for the door to open. We measured Sir's progress toward us by Rex's barks and Sir's occasional guttural commands. Savannah's knuckles turned white as they tightened around my fishnet tights, ready to smash the can into his head. I stood with my open hands in front of my face, elbows in, mentally trying to rehearse all the kung fu moves she'd just shown me.

While I'd been hitting the pillow, I'd felt confident and strong. Every time I heard Savannah grunt when I landed a blow or watched her stagger backward under my assault, it had given me a false sense of security.

But as the moment crept closer when I was going to have to actually try my moves, I started to realize how ridiculous it was to believe that I could damage Sir. Hurt the man who could fill me with fear with just one look from his icy blue eyes.

"*Hier! Fuss! Platz!*" Sir ordered. He sounded inches away. Suddenly the metal and plastic wall separating us from him seemed as insubstantial as cling film. My stomach bottomed out as I waited for the chain to rattle as he unlocked it. My pulse slammed in my ears.

The next sound was the crunch of gravel, but it wasn't on the other side of the door. Instead it came from underneath our feet. I stared into Savannah's wide blue eyes, as puzzled as mine. We were both panting soundlessly through open mouths. I realized I must look like her reflection in a fun house mirror.

And then from somewhere under our feet came the rush of water.

We were still frozen, too scared to move, when the sounds reversed. First the water stopped. Then the gravel crunched under us. Followed by footsteps receding, accompanied by Rex's barks and Sir's commands.

"What did he do?" Savannah demanded in a whisper as Rex's barking faded.

Part of me already knew the answer, but I still hoped I was wrong. After putting the glass under the kitchen faucet, I turned the handle. The first second the faucet gushed solid water, but then it hissed and fizzled as the stream became more and more air-filled. And when the glass was only about three-quarters full, the water stopped altogether.

When I turned, Savannah had her hand over her mouth. Her eyes told me she understood. I resisted the sudden urge to toss the water in her face. If she hadn't caught Sir's eye, if she hadn't resisted when he took her, maybe he wouldn't have done it. Wouldn't have taken the water away.

With a shaking hand, I set the glass down on the counter.

"There's probably still some water in the shower," she said. "And I've heard you can drink the water in the toilet tank."

And there was milk and orange juice in the fridge, and it wasn't summer, so we weren't sweating as much. But the truth was that none of that would ultimately matter. I shook my head. "All that means is it's going to take a little longer." I sank down on the couch and put my face in my hands.

Savannah stayed where she was, the useless can still dangling down her back. "That's it, isn't it? Your face is scarred, and my wrist is broken. Neither of us is what he thought he was getting. I bet he's just going to leave that door locked, and he won't come back for weeks. He won't come back until he's sure we're dead."

How many days could you live without water? Was it three weeks without food but only three days without water? Or maybe it was some other multiple of three. Thirty hours without water?

Ever since I'd been taken, I'd been afraid that something would happen to Sir, a heart attack or an accident. And because no one knew I was here, I would starve to death in this RV.

But I had never dreamed that he would actually choose to let me die.

I didn't know if Savannah was right about why he was doing it, but she was right about what was eventually going to happen.

This trailer would soon become our tomb.

LORRAINE TAYLOR

WHEN THE DOORBELL RANG, I RAN TO IT, HOPING IT WAS NEWS about my daughter. About Savannah.

Instead it was a dark-haired woman. "Lorraine? I'm Amy." She held out a business card. On one side was *In Trevor's Memory*, and the other, *Amy Dowd, Volunteer Victim's Advocate.*

"Can I come in and talk?" she asked.

After a second, I stepped back. Was I doing the right thing? And would Tim mind? He'd gone into work, putting in some overtime. He said he didn't see the point of sitting around the house if there wasn't anything he could do to find Savannah. Besides, he needed the extra money to fix his car.

Amy seemed only a few years older than me, but she might as well have been a different species. A show dog next to a mutt. I could tell her black pantsuit was expensive, and it sure hid her extra weight way better than my wrinkled scrubs with a drawstring waist.

"In Trevor's Memory is affiliated with the National Center for Missing and Exploited Children. It was started by the family of Trevor Strider. Maybe you remember him?"

The feeling of unreality was so great that it was like I was watching myself nod. Anyone alive twenty years ago knew who Trevor Strider was. Six-year-old Trevor had disappeared from his front yard in Cedar Rapids, Iowa. He'd never been found.

"Can I sit down?" After I nodded, Amy took Tim's recliner, and I sat on the couch. Tim's sweatshirt was thrown over the chair. The coffee table was covered with mail, dirty plates, and an open pizza box that still held a curling slice. I looked for judgment on Amy's face. But all I saw was barely concealed pain. And somehow that was worse. This was the life I had made for myself, for me and my daughter.

"Anyway," she continued, "I'm here to help, if you want. I'm not law enforcement, although I've worked with them many times, and they're the ones who notified us. I'm not a counselor, but I've been to counseling and learned a lot from it. I'm mostly just here because I've been in your shoes. My daughter, Jenny, disappeared nearly a year ago."

Her words hit me like a blow. "What happened?"

In a few sentences, she sketched out the story of Jenny's disappearance from a tanning salon. Then she switched topics to what she could do for me. "I can assist you in getting the word out, help you deal with the media, set up a website, or whatever else you need. And I know about resources you can use. There's a print shop downtown that will make missing posters for free. And there's a fraternity at Portland State that might distribute them as a community service project."

This was all going so fast. Just hearing Amy list everything she seemed to think I should be doing was overwhelming. I tried to find something to hold on to. "Wait. Your daughter. Jenny. Did they ever find her?"

Amy looked down at her black pumps with their sensible two-inch heels. "No."

"So you don't know what happened to her?" Even though I was sitting on the couch, I felt like I was falling.

This time she looked at me. Her eyes were the color of old ice. "No."

"How do you live with that?" The words burst out of me.

"I won't lie to you. Of course you want your child back. And if you can't have that, then you want a body. When you realize this limbo might go on forever"—she raised her empty hands and let them fall—"it feels unbearable. Only you have to find a way to live with it." She straightened her shoulders. "But it's far too early to be talking about that. What we should be doing is figuring out how to maximize every resource to bring your daughter home. We need as many eyes as possible looking for Savannah."

It was clear she was a much better mother than I had ever been. The best I could hope to do was follow her lead. "Okay."

"The first thing to do is make a flyer and then get it put up all over the metro area." She pulled a sleek silver laptop from her leather bag and set it on her knees. "Do you have a recent photo of her?"

"When Officer Diaz sent out one of those 'be on the lookout for' announcements to all the other cops, he used Savannah's school portrait."

"It would also be good to have a candid photo. Ideally, head and shoulders, with a light-colored background. But it needs to be sharp. So if you don't have one that's suitable, we'll just go with the one from school."

As I scrolled through photos on my phone, I realized how many there were of Tim and how few of Savannah. Again, shame washed over me.

While I searched, Amy asked me questions, gradually reducing my precious daughter to numbers and colors.

I found myself telling her what I never would have told Officer Diaz. "When I was pregnant with Savannah, I could feel her. Do you know what I mean?" I rested my hand on my belly. She stopped typing and almost reluctantly nodded. "Like this little *hum* of connection. And I can still feel it. I know she's alive."

Amy glanced away, blinked rapidly, then looked back at me again. "If that keeps you going, then good. Because you're going to need every source of strength you can draw on." She looked back down at her keyboard. "So have you found a photo?"

I held out my phone. "What about this one?"

It was Savannah the night she got her orange sash. She'd asked someone at her school to take the picture and then sent it to me.

Amy's eyes widened. "My God!"

"What?"

"Jenny's face was more rounded. But she and your daughter—they look a lot alike. And my daughter disappeared only about seven miles from here."

Suddenly it seemed like Jenny's mom and I had something in common after all.

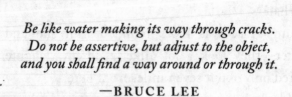

Be like water making its way through cracks.
Do not be assertive, but adjust to the object,
and you shall find a way around or through it.

—BRUCE LEE

SAVANNAH TAYLOR

I STARED AT THE HALF-EMPTY GLASS OF WATER. SIR WAS GOING to let us die of dehydration. It was incredibly cruel. For us, but not for him. He wouldn't even have to get his hands dirty.

I slumped into one of the swivel chairs. Putting my feet on top of the seat, I sat with my face pressed against my knees.

"What are we going to do now?" Jenny sounded close to tears. Water we couldn't afford to waste.

"I don't know." I didn't raise my head. My voice was muffled by my legs. "I don't think there's anything we can do."

"What? You're just going to give up?" Her tone was a challenge.

I didn't raise my head. "Everything you said earlier is

true. There's no way to get out of here. And even if we could, that dog's out there just waiting for us. And even if we somehow managed to get past the dog, then Sir would hear all the barking, realize we're escaping, and then *he'd* kill us." My chest tingled, and there was an ache in the back of my throat.

"But there's gotta be something we can do."

Jenny's words started to reach me. "Whenever I get stuck, I ask myself what Bruce Lee would do." The question echoed and faded inside of me as it went unanswered. "That's where I got the idea for putting the can in your tights, because it was kind of like these nunchucks he used. But I don't think even Bruce Lee could get out of here."

"Bruce Lee—that's the kung fu guy your book's about, right?"

I nodded, then got up and found the book. "It's kind of ironic that his most famous quote is about water."

"What did he say about it?"

I sat next to her. "Something about how you need to be like water, because it's formless. He said that if you put water in a cup, it becomes the cup, or if you put it in a bottle, it becomes the bottle." I started to flip through the book, looking for the quote. Jenny leaned in.

From photo after photo, Bruce Lee stared back at us. His dark gaze was intense, and his thick black hair looked almost like a wig. The muscles in his arms and abdomen were so defined that he could have posed for a medical textbook. In one picture he had parallel red scratches on his cheek as if a beast had clawed him. In almost every photo, he was unsmiling, but then I turned a page and saw him grinning up at me. There was no way to look at that photo without smiling back, at least a little. It was hard to believe that he was dead and had been for almost fifty years.

"When did he die?" Jenny asked.

"Nineteen seventy-three." The word *die* reminded me of our own hopeless predicament. Abruptly, I closed the book. "Maybe Bruce Lee was saying there are times you have to stop fighting and redefine yourself based on your circumstances." I felt like I had stepped up on the railing of a balcony.

"What do you mean?" Jenny's hands twisted in her lap.

I leapt. "I mean—maybe we should just give up. We tried to get out of here, and we failed. Maybe we just have to redefine escape. Why should that creep get to decide how we die?" As I spoke, my voice strengthened. "If I'm going to die no matter what, I'd rather just get it over with." I got up and started toward the bathroom. "Do you have any medication I could use to overdose?" If I was going to do this, it would be best if it was fast and painless.

Jenny came after me. "No, Savannah." She caught my upper arm, her long fingers like wires. "If you kill yourself, then you're just letting him win. And you'd be leaving me alone."

"Then join me. We'll show him that he can't control us the way he thinks."

She shook her head. "I can't kill myself. I used to think about it when I first got here, but I couldn't make myself do it." Her voice was rough with emotion. "And if *you* die, then I'll just be left here alone with your corpse. Do you know how awful that would be?" She wiped drool from her chin. "There has to be some way to get out of the RV. And even if we only make it part of the way and then Rex gets us, you're right. It still beats the alternative." She touched my arm. "Here. Want to know what Bruce Lee would do? Because I think I saw your answer." Retrieving the book, she paged through it until she found what she was looking for.

I read aloud the quote she pointed at. "Defeat is a state of mind; no one is ever defeated until defeat has been accepted as a reality."

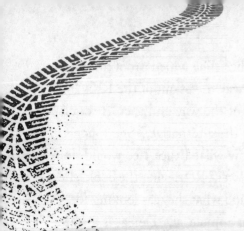

LORRAINE TAYLOR

I JUMPED WHEN THE DOORBELL RANG. IT WAS OFFICER DIAZ, his expression serious. "Can I come in, Ms. Taylor?"

I had called to tell him about Jenny's resemblance to Savannah. But he had sounded busy and distracted, as if their resemblance didn't matter. Now here he was. By his expression, I could tell he did not come with good news. I wanted to freeze this moment, so that time would never move forward. Or erase it altogether.

Instead I gestured him inside, introduced him to Amy. He knew about In Trevor's Memory. She and I sat on the couch while he took Tim's chair. I found myself reaching for Amy's hand. She squeezed back. Her fingers were warm. Mine were like icicles.

"Did you find her?" My voice sounded strangled.

"No. But we do know what happened Thursday night."

He paused, and my heart twisted in my chest. "After she left kung fu class, Savannah was kidnapped by a man who tasered her and then dragged her into a vehicle. A white van."

Each individual word made sense. Savannah. Was. Kidnapped. By. A. Man. Who. Tasered. Her. I just couldn't make the words fit together into a coherent sentence. Things like that happened to other people's daughters. Women you felt sorry for when you saw them weeping on the news.

I finally forced words from my mouth. "Where is she? Is she okay? Who did it? How do you know what happened?"

"There's surveillance video from the parking lot above the kung fu school, but unfortunately it doesn't answer many questions." He held out his hand. On his palm was a flash drive. "Do you have a computer we could watch this on?"

"I've got my laptop," Amy said.

He sat between us on the couch and played the section of video for us. It only lasted a few seconds. Savannah's feet, a man's feet behind hers, Savannah toppling like a tree, a man's hands grabbing her. At the end, what looked like a white van driving past. I sat frozen while he played it again, explaining how the stiff way Savannah fell made him believe she had been tasered.

The third time through, Officer Diaz hit the pause button in the middle. "I want to ask you something, Lorraine."

"Okay." It was hard to force the word past the lump in my throat.

"Do those boots and coveralls look familiar?"

I squinted. The parking lot was dark. The video was blurry. They were far away. Still . . .

"Do you think they might belong to Mr. Hixon?"

I wanted to deny what we were all seeing. "I don't know. But that looks like what he wears to work."

"There's something I haven't told you, Lorraine."

Now I really didn't want to know. "Yes?" I made myself ask.

"Before I came here, another officer and I attempted to question Mr. Hixon about what we saw on this tape."

Dizziness washed over me. I had brought Savannah here. My daughter. "What did he say?"

Officer Diaz pressed his lips together before he spoke. "It did not go well. Mr. Hixon was uncooperative and belligerent. He accused us of trying to 'pin it' on him. But he was also saying something about how it's impossible to know what people are really capable of. He ended up throwing a punch at the other officer. Right now, he's in jail, charged with assault."

"That doesn't sound like Tim," I whispered. Only it did sound like him. "But what about that white van? That's not his. He drives a sixty-eight Camaro. But it's not working right now."

"He's a mechanic, right?"

"It's the parts," I said, misunderstanding what he was saying. "They're hard to get."

"Does he have access to vehicles customers leave at the shop?"

"I guess he would."

"Has he shown any unusual interest in your daughter?"

Bitterness coated the back of my tongue. I didn't think it was possible, but things had just gotten worse. "No." Was that really true? She and Tim were home alone together every night while I was at work. And Savannah had made no secret of not liking him. I had thought it was just because he was rough around the edges.

Officer Diaz continued. "Did you know Mr. Hixon was once arrested for domestic violence?"

"What?"

"Fifteen months ago, he was arrested for assaulting a woman who also occupied this residence. But rather than cooperate with the DA, she moved away." He paused. "At least that's what we thought happened at the time. We are currently having trouble locating her."

Slowly, I filled in what he wasn't saying. Had Tim done something to his last girlfriend to prevent her from testifying? I remembered how he had apologized when he saw the marks on my wrist. How he had kissed them. But he was the one who had made them. Who was he, really?

"Does Mr. Hixon own a Taser?" Officer Diaz's voice seemed like it was coming from far away.

"Not that I know of."

But what did I really know? I was starting to think: nothing.

"Do you mind if we look around? See if we find anything?"

"No." A voice inside me was shouting that I was responsible for this. "Go ahead."

"Is there any area of the house that's off limits to you?" Officer Diaz asked as he got out his cell phone. "Or where he's told you not to go?"

A chill ran over my skin. I shook my head.

Ten minutes later, three more officers arrived and joined Officer Diaz in searching the house. Amy sat with me on the couch, which became an island of calm in a sea of movement. Not knowing what else to do, I played the video over and over. *Were* those Tim's boots? Tim's hands roughly grabbing under Savannah's arms?

I realized Amy was shaking, an almost imperceptible trembling. We exchanged a glance. Was she thinking what I was? That Tim could have taken both Savannah and Jenny?

When Amy pressed the button to watch the video one more time, I got up to use the bathroom. All the outlet and vent covers had been taken off. "Are you looking for drugs?" I asked one of the new officers, a woman, who was in our bedroom, across the hall.

"No, ma'am." Was I imagining the judgment on her face? "We were looking for hidden cameras."

Hidden cameras? I realized who they thought Tim might have been filming. I tried to keep my voice steady. "And did you find any?"

"Not so far."

I closed and locked the bathroom door. I barely made it to the toilet in time to be sick. How could I have been so blind? What had Tim done to my Savannah?

Ten minutes later, when someone tapped on the bathroom door, I had thrown up so much all that was coming out was yellow bile.

"Lorraine?" It was Amy. I had only met her a few hours ago, but now she knew more about me and my messed-up life than anyone. I was too paralyzed with fear and guilt to feel shame. How could she even stand to talk to me, the woman who had been obliviously living with Tim for months? "Lorraine, can you come out here for a second? Detective Diaz wants to talk to you."

I flushed the toilet, rinsed out my mouth, and unlocked the door. Amy didn't say anything, just took my arm. As we walked down the hall, I felt like a prisoner being led to the electric chair. Had they found Savannah's body?

But the reason was laid out on the dining room table. Two handguns and an assault rifle. All of them a dead, flat black.

"Did you know that Mr. Hixon had these?" Detective Diaz asked.

1. Learn the rules.
2. Keep to the rules.
3. Dissolve the rules.

—BRUCE LEE

SAVANNAH TAYLOR

JENNY WAS RIGHT. EVEN IF OUR SITUATION SEEMED IMPOS-sible, it was wrong to embrace death. So what would Bruce Lee do if he were the one stuck in this motor home? If I had learned one thing about him, it was that he was always seeing things from a different angle. Unlike Sir, he had disdained rigid rules. *Rules.* Something about that idea nagged at me.

I leaned toward Jenny. "What were those stupid rules of Sir's again?"

She took a deep breath and rattled them off. "Always call him Sir. Never look him in the eye. Dress attractively. Keep things picked up. Don't make noise. And be grateful that he keeps you alive."

"Only he's the one who's breaking the last rule." I got up and started pacing. The space was so small I was almost walking in circles. "Maybe we need to break all the other ones. What would happen if we did the exact opposite of them?"

She tilted her head. "What do you mean?"

"Take the one about not making noise. What if we opened the door as far as it goes and started yelling? Then Rex would start barking. And if Sir came back to tell us to be quiet, we could attack him." An even better idea bloomed. "Or, wait a minute. Technically, this is a vehicle, right? Which means it has a horn. What if we started honking it?"

Jenny's broken mouth smiled. "Oh, Sir wouldn't like that. Not at all. He'd get nervous someone would hear and start asking questions." Her expression changed. "But couldn't he just cut a wire or something, like how he went underneath and opened up the water valve?"

"I don't think he could open the hood without releasing a latch. And to do that, he'd have to come inside and pull a lever or something under the dash." I leaned over and grabbed up the tights/SpaghettiOs nunchucks. "Once he unlocks the chain, I'll hit him with the can, just like we planned. And then we'll run for the fence."

Jenny's hand rose to her scars. "But what about Rex?"

Another piece of the plan fell into place. "When we start making noise, Rex will start barking, right? And when Sir yells at Rex, we can listen to the commands and then use them ourselves after we escape."

"But Rex will know we're not Sir."

"If it doesn't work, I can always hit Rex with the can, too." I actually felt worse contemplating hurting the dog than I did the man.

"Rex moves so fast, though." Jenny winced. "What if you miss?"

An answer hovered just out of reach, until I thought back to the rules. "Instead of dressing attractively, we'll put on all your clothes. Layer them up. That way, if Rex tries to bite us, he'll just get cloth instead of skin."

"That might work." She looked at my sling. "But how are you going to put layers over that?"

In my excitement, I'd forgotten about it. "I'll take off the sling, but not the splint. Do you have some sweaters or something that would stretch over it?" I figured the magazine would protect my forearm.

Jenny began pulling clothes out of boxes and plastic bags and from the tiny closet and along the walls. Some were simply impractical, like short skirts and dresses. The rest we laid on the bed, making piles of tops and bottoms that went from smallest to largest, trying to figure out which order to put them on in and who would wear what.

She ended up in two pairs of leggings topped with a pair of pants. I could only fit a single pair of leggings under my pants. It was easier to layer tops. With my splint, I was able to get into three, while Jenny wore five. For a final layer, I managed to squeeze into my shredded puffer coat. Jenny didn't even have a coat, just a pink and white kimono. We both looked lumpy and misshapen, like we were going to a crazy costume party.

"We should do something more about your neck," I said, gesturing. I still had my kung fu shirt and the remains of my jacket to provide some protection, but all of the clothes he'd brought her had deep V-necks. We'd both tied hand towels around our necks, but a single layer didn't seem like enough. I snapped my fingers. "Bruce Lee!"

"There's another saying?" she asked.

"No, I mean the actual book." It was a heavy oversized paperback. I handed it to her. "Try sticking it down your front." Shoved down the layers of shirts and sweaters and held up by her bra, it shielded the top of Jenny's chest and most of her throat.

Jenny looked around the RV, now strewn with stuff. "Well, we've certainly broken the rule about keeping things picked up." She managed a smile.

My eyes fell on her plastic boom box. "Wait! What if we used the boom box to record his commands and then play them back after we escape? Rex might believe it's Sir. At the very least, it should slow him down."

We spent the next half hour experimenting. I stood at the driving end of the RV while Jenny stationed herself just inside the bedroom door and held out the silver plastic mic. Even when I switched from a half shout to my normal voice, the attached microphone still did a good job of recording my words.

Finally we turned off all the lights and took our stations. I was standing on one side of the door, while Jenny was sitting in the driver's seat.

"Ready?" I said.

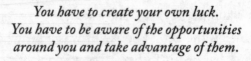

> *You have to create your own luck.*
> *You have to be aware of the opportunities*
> *around you and take advantage of them.*
>
> —BRUCE LEE

SAVANNAH TAYLOR

INSTEAD OF ANSWERING WHEN I ASKED IF SHE WAS READY, Jenny just pressed the horn. It was so loud it hurt my ears. She leaned on it over and over. *Blatt–blatt–blatt.* Then she switched to a pattern. *Blip–blip–blip, blatt–blatt–blatt, blip–blip–blip.* Three short beeps, three long beeps, three short, and then a pause. When she repeated it, I recognized the pattern. SOS in Morse code.

Soon Rex was adding to the noise of the horn, barking so fiercely it sounded like one continuous sound. A few seconds later, his nails scrabbled on the metal steps. I pressed my eye to the crack where the tarp had shifted. It was dark outside and had been for a while. I'd been in this RV for about forty-eight hours, but it already felt like an eternity.

I couldn't yet see Sir, but finally, in between beeps, I heard his shouts.

"He's coming!" Holding the mic and the boom box,

Jenny scrambled into position next to me. With my splint, I was holding the improvised nunchuck against my body. After pushing open the door as far as it would go, I grabbed the end of the tights in my fist.

As the door started to move, Rex's barking reached a crescendo. He thrust his muzzle into the gap between the door and the frame. Behind me, Jenny shrieked, but I didn't budge. Rex futilely snapped his jaws just a couple of inches from my thigh. Despite the cold night air, sweat broke out under my arms and traced my spine.

Sir was coming closer, shouting, *"Hier! Fuss! Platz!"* I prayed that the recorder was catching every word.

At the sound of his master's voice, Rex didn't stop barking, but he did pull his head back.

When I spotted Sir through the gap in the door, I whispered, "Now," to Jenny. We didn't need him guessing what we were trying to do. The recorder landed behind the couch with a muffled thump.

Suddenly Sir was the one with his face in the gap, only much higher than Rex's had been. His breath stank of alcohol.

"You know the rule about making noise!"

"Sorry," Jenny said, without adding *Sir*. Her voice shook as she broke two rules at once, because she was also looking directly at him. "But we need to talk."

"Not right now, we don't. You girls need to be quiet and go to bed. It's late, and I'm tired. We can talk in the morning."

"We're not going to be quiet," I countered. "Not when you're leaving us here to die."

"Listen, girl, don't you ever tell me what to do!" Sir's hand, holding the Taser, shot through the gap. He pressed the end against the hand towel tied around my neck. The air filled with a quick snapping sound. The towel, it turned out, was no protection at all. The pain was indescribable. When I tried to pull away, Jenny was so close that I just stumbled against her.

Desperately, I swung the can over my head as hard I could and down through the gap. A grunt exploded from Sir when it thumped against his back, but he kept pressing the Taser to my neck. I felt the end of the tights slide through my fingers, the weight of it yanking it out of my grasp. But I could only think about the pain, not my lost weapon.

Out of the corner of my left eye, I saw a blur as Jenny smashed the heel of her hand through the gap and into the center of Sir's face. She caught him just under the nose, driving him back.

Sir let out a shriek. The Taser came away from my throat, and he fell backward off the top step. He landed with a curse, but in less than a second, he had scrambled back to his feet. It didn't seem like we had done any damage. And the nunchuck was gone.

"Go ahead," he yelled. "Make all the noise you want. This time of night, there's no one to hear. And if you haven't figured out how to be quiet by morning, I'll *make* you be quiet."

And then he left.

And we were still behind the chained and padlocked door.

JENNY DOWD

AFTER SIR STORMED OFF, SAVANNAH CLOSED THE DOOR AND turned on the light. Both of us squinted against the sudden brightness. She sagged on the couch, her fingers massaging her neck.

Even though our plans hadn't worked, I felt oddly powerful. I had talked back to Sir. Not only that, I had hit him! When I felt his nose shift under my palm, it had unleashed a feeling of savage glee.

Savannah's eyes looked wet. "What do we do now?" she asked. "Should we wait until morning and then honk the horn again?"

Starting to shake from adrenaline, I remembered his threats. "But what if he comes back with a gun?" I moved into the hall. "We got so close with the vent. Maybe there's still a way to get it loose." I jumped up and grabbed the metal crossbar. Above me, the vent let out a groan.

Was it possible to simply yank the screws loose? Fueled by a surge of excitement, I braced my feet on one wall and pulled down so hard my arms trembled, but the vent didn't shift or make any more noise.

Savannah joined me, jumping up and grabbing the bar with her one good hand. But even our combined weight did nothing. Finally we both let go, landing on the floor with a hollow thud.

Her eyes got big. "What's under here?" she asked, bouncing on her toes.

"What do you mean? That's the floor."

"I know that, but what's under the floor? It sounds like there's some kind of open space underneath." Her face lit up. "I'll bet there is! Like where Greyhound buses store the luggage. If we could get down inside it, we might be able to get out."

Hope flared and just as quickly died. "Even if there is a space, we don't have a saw or anything to cut through the floor to get to it."

"But the floor feels spongy. Like it's rotten." She kept bouncing.

I followed her example. She was right. That section of the floor felt squishy. I had noticed it before and then each time promptly forgotten, ignoring it the way I ignored the rest of my circumstances. "Every time it rains hard, water leaks through the vent."

Savannah dropped to her knees. "Let's check it out."

Together, we plucked and pulled at the flat brown carpet, trying to get it loose. I broke a nail past the quick in the process, but I didn't care. We finally managed to yank it back with a ripping sound, releasing the fusty smell of mold.

Savannah was right. Under the vent, the particle-board floor was black and rotting. I grabbed one of the spoons and the spork, and together Savannah and I attacked the rotten wood, side by side on our knees.

It was like digging through a quarter inch of wet, slimy, splintery dirt. The smell of mildew clogged my nose. We started using the handles of our utensils like pry bars, lifting up crumbling chunks of wood. Underneath the layer of rotten particle board was something white. As we uncovered more of it, I realized it was a layer of Styrofoam a couple of feet wide, with metal braces on the edges. After we had exposed about a two-foot length, we gouged at it, wincing at the squeaking sounds the Styrofoam made.

There had to be a faster way. I got to my feet, took a deep breath, and stomped down with my right foot, punching a hole straight through the Styrofoam. I tumbled forward as my foot dropped two feet before finally landing on something solid.

Savannah backed up, took a running leap, and landed with both feet right beside me. With a high-pitched squeal, the entire panel of Styrofoam gave way. We fell in a tangled heap.

And then we were laughing. Laughing and trying to be quiet. I hadn't laughed about anything in ten months.

DANIEL DIAZ

I LEFT THE DENTIST'S OFFICE BEFORE MY DAD DID. HE HAD TO document everything we had found. Before I left, Macy surprised me with an awkward hug. As I was biking home, the memories of what I'd seen on the surveillance video repeated themselves over and over. Savannah being tasered, hitting her head, and then being dragged away. The van rushing past and disappearing.

What had that guy Tim done to her? Where was she? Was she even still alive? My stomach was in knots.

When I got home, the house was quiet. Orlando was at a friend's. My mom was curled up on the couch reading a book, so it was easy to walk past her while only exchanging a few words. Easier than explaining what was really happening. I was starting to see why my dad never shared things.

But once I was in my room, I couldn't stand being alone with my thoughts. I started texting friends, asking if they knew of any other girls who had been followed.

I also started thinking about what had happened in that extra hour before Savannah showed up on the camera. It seemed like a clue, if only I could figure out what it meant. And what about the van? If we could find it, could we find Savannah?

I was pretty sure the first three digits on the license had been SVT. Oregon license plates were a series of three numbers followed by a space and then three letters. Years ago, it had been the reverse—three letters followed by three numbers. So while the surveillance camera had shown just the SVT, a space, and only part of what came next, I knew they would have been numbers.

Which meant there were 999 possible vehicles. A thousand, because there must have also been a SVT 000. But the next digit had looked like it had a straight line at the top. Tracing numbers in the air, I realized that only a five and a seven had that line.

That left only two hundred possibilities. Maybe even a lot less. First of all, how many vehicles were white vans? And second, a plate that started with SVT had to be really old. My mom's car was seven years old, and even it started with three numbers and ended with three letters. It had been a long time since plates had started with letters. So how many white vans were still on the road after fifteen or twenty years?

A couple of hours later, when I heard my dad's car pull into the driveway, I pushed myself off the bed. Part of me was afraid to hear whatever he would say. I started toward the living room, but he met me in the hall. His face was etched with weariness.

"What happened?" I asked before he said anything. "Did you find Savannah?"

He raised one hand. "If I tell you, it's for your ears only. Not to be shared with anyone."

I nodded. "I understand. I won't." Did my dad think I was a little kid?

"Myself and another officer went to speak to Hixon at work. He claimed he didn't know what happened to Savannah and that he didn't have a white van. He also became belligerent and threw a wild punch." My dad pinched the bridge of his nose. "But the most important thing is that he was wearing coveralls and work boots."

Just like the guy in the video. "What happened to him?"

"He's been charged with assault. He was previously arrested for domestic violence, but the charges were dropped after the victim moved away. After he was taken to jail, I showed Ms. Taylor the video. She was pretty sure it was Tim. Then she gave us permission to search the house." My dad paused, then looked me straight in the eye. "We found three guns he'd hidden."

A picture of Savannah shot to death sprang into my head, but I pushed it away.

"Did you find the Taser?"

"Not yet."

"Maybe if we could figure out where Savannah was for that hour-long gap on the surveillance footage, it would help us figure out what happened to her," I suggested.

He waved a hand. "Oh, it's not really a gap. I checked. It's just that the camera was still set on daylight savings time."

Why hadn't I thought of that? "So that white van in the video was his?" I asked.

"Hixon's only car is a 1968 Camaro, which is currently out of commission. So he doesn't own a white van, but he does have access to any vehicle left at the shop overnight or longer. We're checking the shop's records, but it's going to take some time. It's even possible that he's secretly had keys made for vehicles. But if that's his MO, it explains why Courtney and Sara reported being followed by different cars."

I held out my phone. "I've been texting people today. It's happened to more than just Courtney and Sara. There were a couple of girls at the middle school, too. There's, like, a total of five. But the cars sound like they're all different. They only had one thing in common. They were all old beaters."

"Old beaters have to get fixed, too," my dad said. "And eyewitness testimony is notoriously wrong. I've had people swear up and down that white is black. Literally."

"But what if this Tim guy is telling the truth? What if it was a different person in that van? Either way, couldn't you figure out who it belongs to if you worked from the license plate backward through the DMV's records? It started with either SVT five or SVT seven. How many white vans could there be with that plate sequence still on the road? Can't you look it up?"

My dad shrugged. "Color's a nonissue, Daniel. Records

never include the color of the vehicle, since cars can get repainted and there isn't even a standard set of colors. One manufacturer's 'beige' is another's 'champagne.' A license plate is associated with both an owner and a vehicle, and either one of those could change. The car could be sold and the license plate transferred to a new owner. Or, as I believe happened in this case, the plate itself could be transferred to a different vehicle. Because I *did* do some checking. And way back when, there was a ninety-eight Chevy van that had a plate that started with Sierra Victor Tango seven."

"Really?" I felt a spark of hope.

He shook his head. "But it was salvaged six years ago."

"Salvaged?" I echoed. "What does that mean?"

"It was in an accident, and insurance declared it a total loss. It ended up at All Autos junkyard. People have probably been picking it clean ever since. Ms. Taylor said Mr. Hixon went to junkyards looking for parts for his Camaro. He must have taken the plates at the same time. And then he switched them out on a customer's van. He was probably worried about what did end up happening— the plates being caught by a random surveillance camera." He sighed. "Maybe Hixon will fill us in on how it all worked. But first we need him to tell us what he did with Savannah. And right now, he's refusing to even admit he's involved."

The attitude, "You can win if you want to badly enough," means that the will to win is constant. No amount of punishment, no amount of effort, no condition is too tough to take in order to win.

—BRUCE LEE

SAVANNAH TAYLOR

JENNY AND I WERE SITTING ON THE EDGE OF THE RECTANGLE WE had opened up. The lights from the other rooms did not reach very far into the area we had just uncovered under the hall floor. I leaned down and squinted into the shadows. The space between the main floor and the bottom of the RV was about two feet tall. It seemed mostly empty, holding just a few scattered boxes as well as some wiring and pipes.

"I'm going to see if we can get out through there," I told Jenny.

"Be careful! What if you open up a luggage door and Rex is on the other side?"

I got up and took a wooden spoon from the junk drawer. "Then I'll poke him in the eye with this." I tucked it into the back of my pants, stuck my legs over the side of the hole, and wriggled underneath the floor, which was now my ceiling. There wasn't even enough room to get to my hands and knees. Ignoring the grating of my broken wrist and the ceiling scraping along my back, I started to army crawl on my forearms toward the side of the RV.

The air was stale and fusty. I suppressed a sneeze, wondering how it was possible for dust to accumulate in an enclosed space. A second later, all the familiar horrible feelings of claustrophobia began to cascade over me. My palms started to sweat. A zapping sensation ran down my spine. My chest was getting tighter and tighter.

Before I'd been locked in this RV, my claustrophobia had been caused by an irrational fear. Now I truly was trapped in a small space, possibly forever.

All the other times, something inside me had frozen as soon as I felt the panic begin. I had felt so desperate, mentally begging it to go away. But now instead of being paralyzed by fear, I was somehow able to realize that the sensations flooding my body were just that—sensations.

Instead of focusing on taking deep breaths or telling myself it was okay, I decided to stop trying to change the subject. To stop running away from my fears. *Come on,* I mentally taunted the fear. *Is that all you've got? Because I know now that there are way worse things.* A picture came into my head of my claustrophobia as a little yapping dog, ineffectually trying to sound the alarm. *I don't have all day,* I told it. *I mean, you're trying and everything, but can't you make my heart pound even faster? Can't you make my chest feel even tighter?*

And instead of it gripping me harder, the fear begin to

ease off. I imagined the little dog falling silent, confused. My claustrophobia might be done with me, but I wasn't done with it. *Don't stop now*, I told it. *Don't waste my time like that.* But instead I felt it retreat even further.

I realized that claustrophobia was like one of those woven Chinese finger traps. In order to get out, you had to push in.

Inch after inch, I pulled myself forward. Eventually, I located the side of the RV by painfully banging it with the top of my head. Had the sound alerted Rex? I held my breath but didn't hear anything. Running my good hand along the panel, I eventually found a metal bar that moved when I pressed on it. I heard a *snick* and then felt the compartment door unlatch and begin to swing out as fresh air flowed in.

Thank God. We would be able to get out.

I exhaled in relief. I was sandwiched between levels, barely able to move, but the panic that should have gripped me had turned tail and run, no match for reality.

The space was too tight to turn around in, so I had to crawl backward to return to where Jenny was waiting for me, sitting on the edge of the hole.

"There's a door to the outside, and it opens. Let's get ready and go."

I kept the wooden spoon. If Rex attacked us, I could poke his eye or maybe stick it between his jaws. I shrugged on my backpack that held my wallet and sash. Jenny had the boom box with Sir's voice. She also tucked the spork into her back pocket.

And then we both ducked beneath the floor. When

we reached the compartment door, I put my lips against Jenny's ear. This close, I could smell the sharp scent of her sweat.

"Once we get out, we'll make for that fence you saw. We'll be as quiet as we can. If we hurry, Rex might not hear us until we're on the other side." I tried to remember if dogs were nocturnal. I hoped not. "If he does, then play the tape recorder and keep running. And if he attacks, we have to do everything to stay on our feet. Poke him with the spork. Even if it's not that sharp, he's not going to like it. Punch him in the nose. If there's a tree you can climb, climb it. If we can get up over four or five feet, we'll be out of his range."

"But then we'll be stuck there." Jenny's whisper trembled. "And Sir will hear and come out."

"He smelled like he was pretty drunk. If he's anything like my mom's boyfriend, that means he'll be hard to wake up." I hoped Sir was totally wasted. "Things are not going to get any better tomorrow, so we have to get out of here tonight. And at least right now he's probably asleep. Are you ready?"

"I guess." She took a deep breath. "But, Savannah, if I don't make it, you have to tell my family that I love them."

My anger at Sir morphed into sadness for myself. "The same goes for me. If I don't make it and you do, tell my mom that I love her."

JENNY DOWD

SAVANNAH OPENED THE LUGGAGE COMPARTMENT DOOR. COLD,
fresh air flooded in. Moving carefully and quietly, we
crawled out. It felt like we were moving in slow motion,
but at the same time, we couldn't afford to make any noise.
Every nerve ending vibrating, I waited to hear Rex or Sir.
I didn't know which would be worse. Once we were out,
we lowered the cargo door back to its closed position with
almost exaggerated care. Then I helped Savannah to her
feet.

As I did, I looked up. My breath caught. The night sky
was even more amazing than I remembered, like diamonds
sprinkled over black velvet, with a three-quarter opalescent
moon.

We were standing in the muddy clearing I'd last seen ten
months before. Surrounded by the same fifteen-foot-high

row of car carcasses that had been crushed into scrap metal and then piled on top of each other like oversized gray-and-rust-colored bricks. A narrow gravel road, just wide enough for a car, pierced the wall of metal. On it was parked the white van.

The only thing that had changed from ten months earlier was that now the clearing held a second old RV. About a month ago, I had heard a loud engine outside, but the tiny gap over the window hadn't revealed what was happening. Sir must have intended it for Savannah, at least before she broke her wrist.

And past the second RV was the same run-down two-story house I'd seen during my abortive escape attempt. Sir must be in there. I thought of the knife and the Taser on his belt. If he woke up and heard us, he would surely kill us.

As would Rex.

Without any kind of signal between us, Savannah and I both started, madly, to run. The sound of every footfall made me wince. When a frozen puddle shattered into icy shards under my left foot, my heart leapt in my chest.

The multiple layers of clothes made our run more of a waddle. Despite the slow pace, even before we reached the opening in the wall of cars, I was wheezing. I used to run almost every day, but I hadn't had any kind of exercise for ten months. My lungs burned, and my wasted muscles protested. The boom box thumped against my thigh. The only forces powering me were adrenaline and fear.

At first, Savannah was just a few feet ahead of me, but gradually, the distance between us lengthened.

Where was Rex? He could be anywhere. My nerves

were stretched to the breaking point as I swiveled my head and strained my ears, waiting for an explosion of barking. But the only sounds were our breathing and our feet on the graveled road.

And then we were past the wall. Our horizons opened up. We were surrounded by hundreds, if not thousands, of old cars and trucks. They didn't sit in neat, orderly rows, but in clumps and clusters. Hoods were up or gone. Doors missing. Some had no engine at all. Most had no tires.

My steps were slower and slower, both from exhaustion and from having to watch where I stepped. Bits and pieces of cars were strewn everywhere: seats, fenders, bumpers, bed liners, lengths of black rubber tubing, and white plastic reservoirs that had once held fluids.

I heard Rex before I saw him. It wasn't a bark but a continuous growl, low in his throat. The emotion that filled me wasn't fear. It was a hot eruption of terror. Every strategy we'd plotted flew out of my head.

He was galloping straight toward Savannah. His dark eyes were as big as chestnuts. His mouth was filled with teeth and foam.

And then he was on her, leaping the last six feet. Rex's jaws closed on her thigh, and then he started violently shaking his head. He seemed determined to tear her apart. Somehow, probably thanks to kung fu, she was managing to stay on her feet, her free leg dancing back and forth as she tried to stay balanced.

Finally, I remembered the boom box. I stabbed at the button to play the tape of Sir's commands. Before we left the RV, I had turned the volume to its highest level.

Sir's voice suddenly boomed out. *"Platz! Hier! Hier! Fuss!"* Even though I knew it was just a recording, the sound of him so close caused another wave of terror to crash over me.

Rex abruptly released Savannah's leg. My knees went weak with relief. Her plan was actually working.

He raised his head. He looked from me to Savannah and back again.

Too late, I realized what the word in the middle of our recording of Sir was. *Hier.* Pronounced slightly differently, probably spelled differently, but it must have meant "here." As in "Come here."

And then Rex abandoned Savannah for me.

Cease negative mental chattering. If you think a thing is impossible, you'll make it impossible.

—BRUCE LEE

SAVANNAH TAYLOR

AFTER JENNY BROADCAST HIS OWNER'S VOICE THROUGH THE tape player, Rex let me go. Relief flooded my veins, but it was short-lived. He had abandoned me for Jenny. Her eyes went wide as I think we both understood one of the words Sir had meant.

Frantically, she rewound the few seconds of tape and hit the play button again before throwing the recorder a dozen feet away. She must have hoped he would run to it, rather than her.

But Rex didn't swerve, didn't even hesitate, as he hurtled toward her. When he was still six feet away, he leapt.

Jenny screamed then, a wordless sound of utter terror. Rex barreled into her chest, knocking her onto her back. I staggered as fast as I could toward them.

My blood chilled when I saw that he had Jenny's wrist

in his mouth. Growling, he shook it back and forth. I was on them now. I hit his nose with a right hammer fist as hard as I could. It was wet with his spittle, and I felt it give under my blow. But it was as if I had done nothing.

Jenny looked like she had fainted, loose and boneless. Her head lolled back, exposing the top half of her throat, which wasn't protected by the Bruce Lee book.

I needed to try something else. Frantic, I broke off a car antenna and brought it down on the dog's back like a whip. It didn't even give him pause.

It was hopeless. I would never get him off her. Soon Rex would drop Jenny's wrist and go for her throat. And she would die here in the frozen mud, only a few hundred yards from freedom.

I couldn't let that happen.

The wooden spoon was still in my back pocket. I pulled it out and tried to poke Rex in the eye with the handle. But it just landed on his cheek.

Still, it was enough to make him pay attention to me. Letting go of Jenny, he turned and nipped at the spoon, catching it in his powerful jaws. There was a cracking sound. In a single bite, he reduced it to splinters.

Then he turned back to Jenny, his open jaws dripping spit on her slack white face.

I slapped the dog's butt. "Come get me! Come on!" I stuck my face close to his.

He lunged at me. I smelled his rotting breath. His jaws snapped closed a few centimeters from my face. I took a step back. As I had hoped, he followed. Weren't predators hardwired to scan for movement and then chase it?

An unmoving Jenny wasn't as much fun as a person who screeched and ran and leapt.

So I did, running away from Jenny as far and as fast as I could.

But Rex's four legs were faster than my two. And my path had led me into a tangle of cars from which there was no other exit. I turned to face the dog, my back against the rear end of a big green sedan so old it had fins. If he tried to knock me over, maybe the car would hold me up. I held my arms between him and my face. When he attacked, I would try to give his jaws the splint.

I knew all those moves would only buy me time. In the end, they wouldn't save me.

There had to be another way.

The front passenger door of the old car stood open. I threw myself back on the bench seat and started frantically scooting away. My heels alternated digging into the rotting upholstery and kicking at the snarling dog as he followed me. I was thankful for the hours I had practiced kicking the heavy bag in kung fu.

When my back hit the door, I groped behind me until I found the handle. I opened it while at the same time giving one last kick to the dog's chest. It not only pushed him back, but it also propelled me out the door. I landed on my butt. I rolled under the door and then, lying flat, kicked it closed. Barking, Rex lunged at the window, single-minded in his pursuit.

I pushed myself to my feet, ignoring the pain in my wrist. Putting my face close to the glass, I taunted the dog with my proximity. As Rex threw himself against it, I hoped the window was as unbreakable as the one in the RV.

And then before he could turn around, I ran to the other side of the car and slammed the passenger's-side door shut.

The dog was trapped.

Rex's growls began to alternate with barks. They were only partly muffled by the confines of the car. We had to get out of here before Sir showed up. I turned back to find Jenny.

She was sitting up, looking dazed. With my good hand, I reached out for her. "Come on, Jenny! Get up! We need to go. Now!"

JENNY DOWD

"YOU'RE BLEEDING," SAVANNAH SAID.

When Rex attacked me, I'd stopped thinking. Even now that he was penned up in the car, every bark made me flinch. My whole body was coated with sweat, my heart was thumping in my ears, and my mouth tasted sour.

Savannah was wiping blood from her good hand on her pants. But it wasn't her blood. It was mine. It was coming from my right wrist. The white skin just past the layers of clothes now had a dark hole in it, about as big around as a pencil. Blood was steadily leaking from it. When I turned it over, on the other side was a matching bloody hole.

Looking at it, I could sense my wrist was throbbing. At the same time, it didn't really feel like *my* wrist or hand. It was now just this weak, useless appendage attached to my body.

With her good hand, Savannah pulled the towel from around her neck. "Here, help me tie this around your wrist to stop the bleeding."

Together the two of us managed to tie a bulky knot directly over one of the holes. I barely registered the pain as she snugged the towel taut.

"Try to hold your wrist above your heart," she said. "That will slow down the bleeding."

I knew enough to nod at her words, but they were more a jumble of sounds than anything that made sense.

"We need to get out of here! That dog won't shut up. He'll wake up Sir for sure."

Sir! That did get through to me. Cradling my wrist to my chest, I began to stagger forward in my best approximation of a run. I hadn't walked more than a few steps in ten months, and I was already exhausted from getting as far as we had. Soon my muscles were trembling again, my lungs protesting.

As fast as we could, we traversed the graveled, potholed road toward the fence. A squat cinder-block building sat just on the other side. The junked cars were beginning to be in neater rows, and they looked newer and more complete.

Finally we reached the fence. It was at least ten feet high. A pair of gates made of the same chain-link material as the fence bisected the road. A heavy chain bound the gates together, fastened with a padlock. Like the fence, the gates had metal pipes running the length of the top, middle, and bottom. To help the gates hold their shape, a fourth pipe went diagonally from corner to corner.

The chain-link was already a formidable barrier, but

both the gates and the fence were topped with four strands of barbed wire.

"How are we going to get over that?" Just looking at the wicked inch-long barbs, I felt overwhelmed. I was shaking from the cold, the running, and the fear flooding my thoughts.

"Just start climbing!" Savannah ordered. "I'll figure out what to do about the barbed wire."

Raising my hands over my head, I hooked my fingers into the wires of one of the gates. I ignored how the movement made my wrist bleed more. But when I tried to put the toe of my shoe into the links, it didn't fit. I kicked off my shoes and then stepped up with one foot and then the other. I looked down. I was now a whole ten inches above the ground.

Reaching up with one hand and then the next, I transferred to higher handholds. Now it was time to climb my feet up, too. Leaning back, I pulled out one foot and set it higher up. Slowly, I followed it with my second foot. But the wasted muscles in my arms were barely cooperating. They wobbled and shook every time I shifted my weight.

I looked down. For all the effort it was costing, I was still only a couple of feet above the ground.

And then from behind us, I heard a shout.

DANIEL DIAZ

I TRIED TO SLEEP, BUT IT WAS IMPOSSIBLE. IT SOUNDED LIKE even Savannah's mom believed that her boyfriend, Tim, had taken her daughter. And what could be more damning than your own girlfriend believing that you were the bad guy?

But I couldn't shake the feeling that my dad and the other cops were taking all the puzzle pieces and forcing them together.

If Tim had taken Savannah, then it had to be because of their fight, because she had made him mad. In other words, the reason would be personal, rooted in their relationship. But if that was so, why would Tim also be following girls he didn't know? I'd read about serial killers who started with a family member and then moved on to the wider world, but this was the opposite situation.

And there was something else. *Someone* else. Jenny

Dowd, the girl who had disappeared from Island Tan in Beaverton ten months ago. One of the people I'd texted had reminded me about her. When I looked her up online, it turned out she looked like Savannah. And so did Courtney and Sara. It sounded like the girls at the middle school also had a similar look. All of them with long dark hair, pale skin, and blue eyes.

My dad had said that the totaled van with the license plate SVT 759 had ended up at All Autos salvage yard. Giving up on sleep, I got up and googled it. The pictures online showed hundreds of cars and trucks. Some looked new, others were stripped husks.

The Google reviews gave it an average of two and a half stars. It seemed like people loved the selection and hated the owner.

"This is not one of those places where you can pull your own parts. You can't even go look at the vehicles you want parts from. The place was dead. Why couldn't the guy at the counter have walked me back to see the condition of the vehicle that the part was coming off of? Possibly a company policy, but I didn't see it stated anywhere. It's a very small thing, but I won't do business again there because of it."

"While the selection was good, the owner . . . not so much. If I could rate it negative stars I would."

"Owner was a real jerk. I wanted to go out and look at the vehicle, and he started screaming at me that it was his property and I needed to get off of it."

Next to the last review was a photo of a man standing in front of a cinder-block building. One hand was raised in a fist, and the other was pointing at the viewer. He appeared to have been photographed in midrant. Just some middle-aged white guy with a bald head.

Even though the reviews didn't give his name, suddenly I knew who he was.

A guy who did not want anyone on his property. A guy who would have access to all different kinds of beater cars. Who could probably fix cars even after they had been declared a total loss.

The guy who had been following girls.

The guy who had taken Savannah.

What if I woke my dad? Would he believe me if I tried to explain my thinking? He already seemed certain he knew the answer. And even if it was possible to convince him otherwise, how long would that take? It had been more than forty-eight hours since Savannah was taken.

So even if she was still alive, how long would that be true?

If Savannah was to have any kind of chance at all, it felt like I had to be the one to give it to her. I could go out there, look for the white van. Look for her. Even look for signs of a grave. If I didn't find Savannah, I still might be able to find evidence to convince my dad.

My parents were in bed. But they always left their keys on hooks near the front door.

Moving through the house on tiptoe, I grabbed a flashlight and then the keys to my mom's car.

Not failure, but low aim, is the crime. In great
attempts it is glorious even to fail.

—BRUCE LEE

SAVANNAH TAYLOR

AS JENNY SLOWLY CLIMBED HIGHER, I TRIED TO FIGURE OUT
how we could get over the barbed wire without getting
hurt. Or at least not too hurt. While there were gaps on
the sides of the gates where they connected to each other
and the fence, they were only a couple of inches wide.

The barbed wire wasn't completely taut. Some of the
strands sagged in the middle. The kung fu sash in my
backpack! I could throw it over the barbed wire and then
pull the ends down and back. That might compress the
wires enough for Jenny to climb over. And then she could
do the same for me.

But even as I pictured it, I realized it wouldn't work.
After Jenny went over, the sash would still be on this side
and she would be on the other.

What about the Bruce Lee book currently stuffed down

Jenny's shirt? Could we lay it on top of the barbed wire? But it wasn't big enough, and it was too stiff. It would only protect us from the top strand. We needed something that would drape over all of them.

And then the solution hit me. We were surrounded by cars. Cars with *floor mats*. Ducking into the nearest car, I grabbed the floor mat from the front passenger side. Made of carpet with a rubbery backing, it folded easily when I tried to bend it.

But there was no way I could climb the fence while holding on to the mat. Not with a broken wrist. With my bad hand, I pulled the bottom of my coat away from my other layers, then shoved the mat under and up so that it covered my torso. The stiff top edge pressed against my throat, right where Sir had held the Taser. He would surely do much worse if he caught us. That thought made me hurry to the fence.

Jenny had only made it about three feet off the ground. In fact, she had stopped climbing and was simply clinging to the fence, trembling so hard I could see it from several feet away.

"Come on, Jenny. Keep going!" I grabbed the fence next to her with my good hand and tried to step up, but I couldn't get any purchase. Seeing that Jenny had toed off her shoes, I did the same. Then I jumped as high as I could. Like a monkey, I grabbed with my toes as well as my right hand. The mat threatened to slide loose, but I clamped it against my torso with the elbow of my bad arm. And then I kept clambering.

I had gotten about halfway up when there was a shout behind us. Sir was awake, and he knew we were gone.

We both shrieked in response. I had thought all my adrenaline was used up, but I could feel more flooding me.

Jenny turned to me, her face as pale as a ghost's. "He's going to catch us and kill us."

"No, he's not." I tried to sound like I believed it. Moving as fast as I could, I stepped up one foot and then the other, clinging to the fence with my good hand. "Come on! Don't stop. We are getting over this fence now!" I pushed up hard with shaking legs as I reached for a new handhold.

When I looked over, Jenny hadn't made much progress. The pale green hand towel I had tied around the dog bite now looked black. How much blood had she lost? How much could she afford to lose?

And how long until Sir came for us? My head was on a swivel as I looked from Jenny to the gravel road and back again.

"I'm sorry." Her voice broke. "I'm not strong enough."

"Yes, you are. Look! Just take one more step up and then you can stand on that metal cross pipe." Encouraging her helped me to ignore my own pain, to keep moving up myself.

Trembling, she did as I said.

"That's excellent. You're almost there. Now just reach your right hand up. Good. And now your left. We have to get over this fence before he comes."

Even one-handed, I made it to the top before Jenny. Holding on to the metal pipe, I considered the strands of barbed wire. I needed to put the floor mat over them— and I also needed to hold on to the fence. To do both of those things was going to take two hands, even if one of them wasn't working right. Jenny was clearly in no shape to help me.

I grabbed the top horizontal pole with my left hand, ignoring the grating jolt of pain from my broken wrist. With my right, I tugged the floor mat free of the sweatshirt. I had planned to put the narrowest part over the strands. Now that I was looking at the barbed wire, the mat seemed far too narrow. How could we hold on to it while also getting our legs over? Shifting my grip, I laid the mat down lengthwise. Then I pressed with all my might, making the wires dip.

Jenny was finally even with me. "You go first," I told her. "Grab the mat with both hands and pull it down as hard as you can." The barbed wire groaned when she put her weight on it, giving even farther. "Okay. Push on your toes and straighten your elbows. Good! Now swing your right leg wide and put it to the other side."

But when she tried to push up, Jenny's elbows buckled. After months of being locked away, she was simply too weak.

The sound of a motor made me jerk my head in the direction we had come from. An engine revved.

My heart crammed into the back of my throat as the white van came roaring out of the wall of crushed cars. It was heading straight toward us. The headlights blinded me.

I had thought he would come for us on foot.

But this was worse. He was going to run us over.

The past is no more; the future not yet. Nothing exists except the here and now. Our grand business is not to see what lies dimly at a distance, but to do what lies clearly at our hands.

—BRUCE LEE

SAVANNAH TAYLOR

I TOOK A DEEP BREATH AND THEN LOCKED MY TEETH, PREPAR-ing myself as best I could. With my left hand, I reached down, grabbed the back of Jenny's pants, and hauled her up. The pain from my broken wrist was like a bolt of lightning that ran from my arm to my shoulder and then shot all through my body. The edges of my vision went dim.

But with my help, Jenny was able to straighten her arms and then lock her elbows. She threw one leg over the top of the fence and started to switch her grip.

I looked back. Horror swamped me. The white van was only a few yards away, its engine whining as it went faster and faster.

"Jump!" I yelled at Jenny.

She threw her other leg over the floor mat and then let

go. Somehow she managed to land on her feet. She took one staggering giant step, two, and then sprawled like a rag doll.

Before I could even try to get over the gate, the van slammed into it. Just before my right foot would have been hit by the windshield, I pulled it up and out of the way. The chain locking the two gates together exploded. Both halves slammed back as if thrown open by a giant.

In a split second, desperately clinging to the metal pole at the top of the gate, I was spun one hundred eighty degrees. The gate slammed into the fence on the other side with so much force that it flung me loose. I landed hard on my butt, but I barely felt it. Instead, I scrambled to my feet and turned around. Had the van run over Jenny? I couldn't see her, just the rear of the van and the red flare of its brake lights. Then the driver's door banged open and Sir leapt out.

He spotted me. Lowering his shaved head like a bull, he ran straight at me.

I screamed as he dove at my legs. Too late, I tried to kick him. Before I could, Sir's arms wrapped around my knees. He yanked my legs up, flipping me on my back. He didn't loosen his grip as he slid his hands back to my ankles. After turning me in a half circle, he began dragging me back inside the salvage yard, ignoring my attempts to kick myself free. Sir was a black cutout against the spray of stars. Their light had traveled millions of miles to reach us. And despite their glow, those stars could have died thousands of years ago.

Just like I probably would tonight.

Once we were away from the fence, Sir threw my legs down, then stepped over me and sat on my hips. His left hand pinned my right shoulder to the ground. I tried to buck him off, but he was too heavy. The corners of his mouth lifted, but it wasn't a smile. It was a shape he made with his mouth.

He drew his right hand back. Silver suddenly winked at me. The knife.

Sir raised it over his head and then swung it down toward my chest.

Just as if I was blocking a strike in kung fu, I threw up my splinted left arm to deflect it. The tip of the blade caught in the thick magazine, but the force of the blow still made me cry out.

Before he could yank the knife free, I swung my arm back over my head as hard as I could. At the end I snapped my wrist, the way Sifu had taught us to throw a backfist. The move loosened the knife. It flew into the darkness, landing with a clatter on the gravel.

Sir just laughed and reached both hands for my throat instead.

Then someone called from behind him. "Oh no you don't!"

He turned. It was Jenny. I didn't even have time to be relieved that she was still alive. As Sir got to his feet, his hands balled into fists. I struggled to get up.

Jenny held something in her right fist, and now she swung it at his face. He easily stepped back out of the way. She kept slicing it through the air, keeping him at bay. There was silence except for all our breathing and a patter like raindrops that left dark freckles on his face. It was blood being flung off the makeshift bandage on Jenny's wrist.

"What's that you got there, girl?" He laughed, and now I saw what it was. It was the spork. "Oh, Jenny, give me that." He reached out a hand for it, just as she kicked him the way I had taught her in the RV. A scooping barefoot kick between his legs.

With a high-pitched scream, Sir curled over, his hands clutching himself.

But how long would he stay like that? Frantically, I scanned the ground for a weapon. Tangles of wires, molded pieces of metal and plastic and rubber, a seat from a car, a hubcap . . . And then I saw it. A rusted axle. I tried to pick it up with just my right hand, but it weighed at least thirty pounds. With a grunt, I grabbed it up with both hands.

When I turned back, Sir was choking Jenny, shaking her back and forth the way Rex had shaken me earlier.

> *Take things as they are. Punch when you have to punch; kick when you have to kick.*
>
> —BRUCE LEE

SAVANNAH TAYLOR

I IGNORED THE DIZZINESS THAT THREATENED TO SWAMP ME. I didn't feel the pain of my broken wrist. I didn't feel anything but the desire to stop him. Hefting the axle to my shoulder, I swung it at his head like a metal bat.

It connected with a dull *bong* that reminded me of the cast-iron bell Sifu rang to begin kung fu class. Sir let go of Jenny, put both hands to his head, took two steps, and then toppled over.

Had I killed him? I decided I didn't really care. Instead of checking, I ran to Jenny. She was on her knees, gagging and coughing. Her hands rubbed dark marks on her neck.

"Are you okay?"

"I don't know." She looked at me. Her eyes were wide and wet. "But we got him, didn't we? We got him, Savannah. We're free!"

I was just starting to return her smile when she fell over sideways. I dropped to my knees next to her. Her eyelids were flickering. She was still breathing, even though it was shallow and fast. Had he hurt something in her throat? Cut off oxygen long enough that it had affected her heart or brain?

I looked from Jenny to Sir and back again. I had to get her out of here and to a hospital. But I couldn't risk him following us. Given another chance, he would surely kill us.

I ran back to him. He still hadn't stirred. I grabbed both his feet, tucked them under my good arm, and dragged him on his back to the nearest car, just as he had dragged me earlier. He was completely limp, his head bouncing over the gravel. His left temple was bleeding, leaving a streak on the dirt. I used the kung fu sash from my backpack to tie his hands behind his back and to the car's bumper. My swollen left hand worked only reluctantly. I had to use my teeth to tighten the knots. He was still breathing, but it sounded rough and raspy.

Then I ran back to Jenny. She lay where she had fallen, but now her eyes were at half mast.

"Come on, Jenny, we have to get out of here."

She tried to move, but it was like watching an overturned bug. Her arms and legs just scuffed back and forth in the dirt. Sobbing with exhaustion, I knelt beside her, grabbed her around the waist with my right arm, and somehow managed to get us both to our knees and then to our feet.

"We just have to make it to the van, Jenny. Come on. Stay with me."

Like two drunks, we staggered toward it. A couple of times she started to tip over, but through sheer force of will, I kept her upright.

I opened the passenger door. It was a relief to see the keys dangling from the ignition. The airbags dangled from the dash like deflated balloons. Fine white powder was still floating in the air, like someone had blown flour off an open palm. For some reason, I thought of Bruce Lee blowing Chuck Norris's chest hair at him, and let out a laugh that sounded like a rusty hinge. Somehow I managed to shove Jenny onto the seat.

I slammed her door closed, then ran around the front of the van. The headlights were broken, and the front of the van was dented and scraped from ramming the fence open. The driver's-side door was still open. I dragged myself onto the seat. It was a relief when I started it up without incident. In stockinged feet, I drove past the cinder-block building with a big sign saying ALL AUTOS and out into the empty parking lot. In front of that was a long, lonely stretch of road. I had no idea whether to turn left or right.

I chose right because that was the only hand that worked. It slipped on the wheel as I turned. Resting on my lap, my left hand was throbbing in time with my heart.

I looked over at Jenny. She was slumped against the window. I wasn't even sure she was breathing.

When I looked back at the road, a car was coming straight toward us. As I swung the van back into our lane, I slowed down and started honking the horn, little beeps that I hoped the other driver would understand were a form of communication, not a complaint. Imitating Jenny,

I used the Morse code pattern for SOS. Three short beeps, three long beeps, three short. Still, the car—a dark-colored Subaru Outback—started to pass us.

But the guy driving it looked awfully familiar. Was I just hallucinating after everything that had happened? In the van's sideview mirror, I saw brake lights flash. Then the driver flung his door open and started running back to me.

It was Daniel.

We looked at each other through the driver's-side window. I put my good hand up against the glass, and he matched it with his own.

Then he opened the door.

"Are you all ri—" he started to ask. Then he looked past me and swore. "What's wrong with that girl? Is she alive?"

And when I looked at Jenny's white, still face, I didn't know the answer.

If there is always light, you don't experience light anymore. You have to have the rhythm of light and darkness.

—BRUCE LEE

SAVANNAH TAYLOR

"LEFT REAR ROUNDHOUSE KICK ON MY COUNT," SIFU TERRY said.

I shifted my stance so that my right foot was forward. So did the students in the line on either side of me. Tonight, I was one of three kung fu students testing for purple. Two others were testing for orange. One was Mr. Tae Kwan Do, whose real name turned out to be Jake Clowers. I'd never told him that I had briefly suspected him of being my kidnapper.

Sifu began the count. "One." The five of us kicked into the air and then set our feet back down. "Two . . . three . . . four . . ." As he counted to ten, Sifu and the other black belts observed our kicks, sometimes scribbling a note or leaning over to whisper to each other. Behind us, the room was crowded with higher-ranking students as well as friends and family.

This time my mom was among them. Three months ago, we had moved into a new apartment, partly financed by my half of a GoFundMe account a stranger had set up after Jenny's and my story hit the news.

"Nine," Sifu called out.

My left leg shot out, but as I brought it back, I lost my balance and my toe touched the mat. I quickly moved my foot to the correct starting position. Sifu Terry and at least one other black belt noticed, but I didn't obsess about it. There was a lot I didn't obsess about anymore. I just threw the tenth kick when told to and then waited for the next instruction.

"Go to horse stance." Sifu shifted his gaze to the rest of the room. "I need five helpers with air shields on the mat."

Daniel was the first to respond. Holding the three-foot-long black pad, he stopped in front of me. His expression didn't change, but after spending a lot of my free time with him over the past three months (including winter formal), I could now guess his thoughts. *You got this.*

After calling 9-1-1, he had tried to stop Jenny's wrist bleeding while I begged her to stay strong and with us. Once we got to the hospital, though, it turned out that her recent injuries were not that dire. They gave Jenny antibiotics and a couple of units of blood. They also called in a plastic surgeon to consult about her face. Since then, she'd had two surgeries and was now undergoing laser treatments to reduce the redness of her scars. The plastic surgeon said that even after treatment, there would always be faint white lines on her nose and lip, but her scars were no longer the first thing you noticed about her. Jenny was back at school and also working with a one-on-one tutor her parents had hired to bridge the months she had missed. Her goal was to graduate in June.

At the hospital, my wrist had been reset under local anesthesia. And they replaced the *Real Simple* magazine with a more official splint.

The ER doctor had marveled over how thick the magazine was. "Three hundred ninety-four pages!" She weighed it in her palm. "That's got to be one of the thickest issues they ever printed. If you tried to stop a knife with a current magazine, it'd probably go right through."

Even with my arm in a cast, I had kept coming to kung fu class. Sifu had modified the drills so that I could still participate.

"Right side thrust kicks on my count," he said now. When I turned to my left, I was facing the two students testing for orange. Mr. Tae Kwan Do was no longer on the end. Jenny was. Her counselor had suggested it might be good for her to add to the kung fu I had already taught her that desperate day in the RV. She turned out to be a natural. Her long legs could snap kicks as high as a man's head.

Daniel turned his shoulder to me and braced himself. His arms were threaded through the straps of the four-inch-thick pad that shielded him from shoulder to thigh.

"One," Sifu said. As I drove my foot into the pad just over Daniel's ribs, I didn't hold anything back. He let out a grunt and took a half step back. "Two." Jenny's partner was also having trouble staying in place.

I snuck a glance over my shoulder at the audience. Jenny's brother, Blake, was in the front row of folding chairs, sitting next to his parents. Amy and Bob Dowd were sitting together, with eyes only for their daughter. Jenny had said that her dad had moved home the week before.

A few seats down from them was Officer Diaz, Daniel's father. Daniel had told me that he and his dad had some long talks after Daniel found us. Last week, I had watched *Enter the Dragon* at his house with his whole family. And when his dad caught us kissing in the kitchen when we were supposedly making popcorn, the three of us had all pretended that he hadn't seen anything.

One person not in the room was Tim. My mom still saw him every now and then, but she no longer called him her boyfriend. She had told me a few things about his past that made me feel sorry for him. Last month, she passed on a handwritten note. In it, Tim apologized for his behavior and said he was in anger management counseling. He wrote that he was trying to learn what it meant to be a man. For her part, my mom was attending Co-Dependents Anonymous, which said that true happiness couldn't come from another person.

She'd also promised that we wouldn't leave Portland while I was still living at home. Because of the GoFundMe, I would have enough to make at least a start at college.

Sir, whose real name was Milton Thorne, was in jail awaiting trial. He'd had a fractured skull, but he'd healed up, just like me and Jenny. Everyone seemed certain he would receive a prison sentence so long that he would never get out. After we escaped, the police had searched the wrecking yard he owned for hidden graves, but they had turned up no evidence of earlier girls. It seemed Jenny had been his first and I was his last.

Milton might have been going to prison, but Rex was getting out. A rescue group in upstate New York that specialized in rehabbing vicious dogs had offered to take him. Despite what Rex had done to her face, Jenny hadn't objected. The dog was what Milton had made him. Maybe he could be unmade, and maybe he couldn't. But it didn't seem fair not to give him a chance.

Sifu Terry clapped his hands. "Thank you, helpers. You may salute off the floor. And those of you who are testing should go to horse stance." Then he and the other black belts left the room to confer.

I spread my feet and settled down into a low horse stance, my arms held up as if ready to block an imaginary blow. From my previous test, I knew the black belts would not come back for at least five minutes, long enough that my legs would be trembling.

But I was sure that they would stand up to the challenge. And I was also sure that when the black belts returned, Jenny and I would both be awarded rank. Without turning my head, I managed to catch her eye.

And then we grinned.

ACKNOWLEDGMENTS

THIS BOOK GOT STARTED WITH A REAL AND TERRIFYING EVENT. A few years ago, an ex-con who had already kidnapped one young woman began stalking girls in my neighborhood. He was confronted by our local school resource officer and ended up in a gunfight—right in front of my martial arts school. It seemed like the plot of one of my books come to life. I immediately started wondering what would have happened if he had tried to take one of our students hostage.

So many people helped me pull this book together.

Sifu Wally Jones, who holds a black belt in kung fu, has been my teacher in various martial arts and self-defense techniques for nearly a decade.

Robin Burcell, a retired cop and author in her own right, explained many aspects of police procedure. Julia Rico, an officer in Portland Police Department's Juvenile Runaway Unit, answered my questions about what would happen if a teen was a possible runaway. A former FBI agent and current police officer who preferred not to be named answered my questions about Tasers.

Rich Hoyt, coordinator of Portland's Derelict RV Towing Program, gave me a tour of dozens of impounded RVs. He proved to be a person with a lot of heart—and he was also great at brainstorming how to hold a captive in an RV, as well as how said captive could escape.

Building on what Rich taught me, Karen Pfundtner, whose blog is called *RVing: The USA Is Our Big Backyard*, was willing to answer weird questions from a stranger about escaping from a padlocked RV when you have no tools. She even sent me photos.

Kevin Beckstrom, public information officer for the Oregon Department of Transportation, explained how license plates and registrations work. Kevin has answered research questions for me since my very first book in 1999!

Sam Naficy, MD, FACS, a plastic surgeon in Seattle, has done amazing reconstructive work on people who have suffered horrific dog-bite wounds. He cheerfully answered questions about my imaginary victim while walking his own dog early one morning.

The folks at Sherwood's Pick-n-Pull let me tour their yard and gave me some tips on things my character might find lying around that could be used as weapons.

The Bruce Lee exhibit at the Wing Luke Museum of the Asian Pacific American Experience reminded me why Bruce Lee is considered the best martial artist of all time.

Even I find it hard to believe, but this is my twenty-fourth book with my agent, Wendy Schmalz.

My editor, Christy Ottaviano, helped me dig down deep and make this book even better. I feel lucky that I got to start working with associate editor Jessica Anderson at the beginning of her career. Morgan Rath can coordinate events across a half-dozen states without breaking a sweat. Mallory Grigg and Angela Jun designed the amazing cover. Other wonderful folks at Henry Holt include Lucy Del Priore, Melissa Croce, Katie Halata, Jennifer Healey, Catherine Kramer, Molly Ellis, and Allison Verost.

BRIDGET AND HER MOM ALWAYS FOUND REFUGE in R. M. Haldon's epic fantasy series, Swords and Shadows, while Bridget's mom was losing her battle with cancer. Since then, Bridget has been Haldon's most devoted fan. At one of his rare book signings, Bridget impressed him with her encyclopedic knowledge of his fantasy world. She has been working for Haldon ever since, as he attempts to write the final book in his blockbuster series. But now Bridget can't get in touch with Haldon, and she's the only one who seems concerned. Can she piece together Haldon's cryptic clues and save him before it's too late?

Keep reading for an excerpt.

BOB

The Gun

The gun looked real. No orange tip, no obvious seams where molded plastic pieces had been glued together.

Although who was Bob kidding? He could tell a dirk from a stiletto, but modern weapons were a mystery.

Besides, the important thing about this gun was that it was pointed at his chest. The end of the barrel was just a few inches from his heart. Adrenaline jolted through him.

"Get in the trunk," the young man ordered.

Bob raised his hands in a placating gesture. "Please, Derrick. I just—"

"Shut up," Derrick barked. "I don't want to hear another word out of you, understand?"

"But—"

The word hadn't even left Bob's mouth before the butt of the gun connected with his temple.

Bob's last, half-formed thought was that the gun certainly *felt* real.

BRIDGET

Compelled to Change by an Outside Force

Queen Jeyne regarded the assassin," a voice murmured in Bridget's left ear. "'You must find the babe, and you must kill it. Or you and your family will die screaming.'"

Belatedly, Bridget realized Mr. Manning was eyeing her. She straightened up and looked at him attentively. She resisted the urge to check if her hair completely covered the single earbud and the short stretch of wire that disappeared under the collar of her shirt. Normally it wasn't hard to listen to an audiobook and a teacher simultaneously, but physics was sometimes challenging.

"While it's true that a falling apple got Isaac Newton thinking about gravity," Mr. Manning said, "there's no evidence one hit him on the head. But he did start wondering why apples always fall down, rather than sideways or even up."

He still seemed focused on Bridget, so she tried to look intent as he explained how Newton had postulated that everything in the universe was attracted to everything else in the universe. Calculating the degree of attraction required a complicated formula, but it basically depended on how far apart the two objects were, as well as their mass.

Walker's stage whisper came from the last row, perfectly pitched to reach the other students but not Mr. Manning. "If that's true, then how come I'm not attracted to fat girls?"

As the offensive comment earned him a few snorts, Bridget exchanged an eye roll with Ajay, one row over.

Sensing trouble, Mr. Manning began to roam the aisles as he talked about mass and universal gravitation. Bridget's attention soon returned to the fine thread of sound connecting her to another, far more interesting, world.

The audiobook's narrator had moved on to the hunt for the baby. In her mind's eye, Bridget was beside the assassin as he snuck down an alley. Together they looked up, trying to spot foot- and handholds in the rough wall. Once he climbed into the attic room, the assassin planned to kill Jancy, the newborn baby now lying in the arms of her mother, a serving girl named Margarit. It was Margarit's misfortune that one night, nine months ago, she'd caught the king's eye. And that a seer had prophesied one of the king's children would grow up to overthrow him.

The only solution seemed to be to order the murder of his own offspring, but the king had balked. When it came to his illegitimate children, Queen Jeyne was not nearly as squeamish.

"Newton began developing the laws of motion when he was only twenty-three. Just six years older than you guys," Mr. Manning said. "Derrick, can you tell me the first law of motion?" He liked to randomly call on students.

Derrick, a tall, skinny guy with a bad complexion, straightened up. Bridget had never talked to him, but she knew who he was. Everyone at school did—for all the wrong reasons.

"Basically, it says a body at rest will remain at rest, and a body in motion will remain in motion, unless they are compelled to change by an outside force."

Walker made a sotto voce comment about bodies in motion, but Bridget paid no attention. The book was approaching one of her favorite scenes. The voice in her ear painted a picture of a cramped room, barely big enough to hold a straw-stuffed mattress. The low ceiling forced the assassin to stoop as he crept forward. The image was so vivid that Bridget reflexively hunched her shoulders. On the bed a sleeping Margarit lay curled around her baby. She was a long-legged, milk-white girl of some six-and-ten years. A healthy wench, to look at her. At least, the narrator warned, she would be until the assassin's dagger entered her heart.

A dagger. Was this dagger in the database? Bridget jotted in the notebook hidden under her classroom notes. R. M. Haldon's fantasies were famous for the wide variety of weapons the characters wielded, from dirks to double-bladed axes to the misericorde, a long narrow knife used to deliver a merciful death to gravely wounded knights.

Even though she was focused on the details, the overall story still enthralled Bridget. It didn't matter that she'd heard or read it more than a dozen times before. That she knew how the assassin's mission would fail, or how the blind seer's prophecy would come true in surprising ways.

Bridget was so enraptured that she didn't notice Mr. Manning had stopped speaking. Didn't glimpse him creeping up behind her. Didn't hear Ajay's frantic throat clearing.

And then the teacher's fingers plucked away her earbud. She let out a shocked bleat as he held it out of reach, the wire stretched tight.

"Hand me your phone," Mr. Manning ordered.

She slipped her phone from her pocket. In order to give it to him, she had to pop the earbud wire from the jack. When she did, the narrator's plummy tones suddenly filled the classroom.

His dagger was poised to plunge into the sleeping girl, when to his surprise, he saw a knife glinting in her left hand. The blade was as thin as she was. Then the point was under his chin, pressing his head up.

"Drop it," Margarit said calmly. When he did not comply, she twisted her own blade. The babe whimpered as a trickle of blood, looking more black than red, dripped onto its skin. She whispered, "Sleep, Jancy."

The assassin—

Mr. Manning stabbed a button on her phone, and it mercifully fell silent. "Was that *King of Swords*?" he asked, incredulous. It was clear he'd expected to hear a popular song, not a book published before Bridget was born.

Its age didn't stop anyone from enjoying it now. Haldon lived in a Portland suburb, but people all over the world had read *King of Swords*, its sequels, or the graphic novel adaption, or at least seen the spin-off TV show.

Bridget nodded. Her cheeks were on fire. She cursed her redhead's complexion for betraying her. She'd been caught on her phone before, but at least then no one had known exactly what she was listening to. Were people now going to lump her in with Derrick, known school-wide as the weird loner who spent his weekends live-action role-playing—LARPing—in a game inspired by Swords and Shadows? Because while it was mostly fine to be a fan, there was an unspoken line, and once you were perceived to have crossed it, you became a socially inept, geeky pariah.

Behind her, Walker was saying something about "queen of kooks," but Bridget ignored him.

She sat in miserable silence until class ended and Mr. Manning handed her phone back. As she gathered her things, Ajay leaned over.

"All that trouble just for a book?" He raised one eyebrow, but his dark eyes were friendly. Whenever Mr. Manning or Walker was being unbelievably annoying, they would trade glances and the occasional whisper.

"It's not just *a* book." She lowered her voice as Derrick walked by. She was relieved that he wasn't seeking her out. "It's *King of Swords* by R. M. Haldon."

"Those books always look so thick." With his fingers, Ajay measured a space about four inches high. "And I'm not a big reader."

"You haven't even seen the TV show?"

He shrugged.

"You have no idea what you're missing."

"Want to fill me in over lunch?"

For a moment, Bridget forgot about the assassin, Margarit, and Jancy. She forgot to think at all. There was only Ajay, standing close enough she was aware of the warmth emanating from his skin and the faint smell of ginger on his clothes. Ajay, with his thick black brows and friendly dark eyes. Ajay, who had been whispering little asides to her all fall. Ajay, who was now shifting from foot to foot, waiting for her answer.

If she were a character, what would she do? Simper? Flirt? Turn down Ajay and leave him disconsolate? More than nearly anyone in the world, Bridget could imagine how she might handle this situation if it were fictional.

But it wasn't. And she wasn't a queen or a peasant girl or a courtesan. She was just Bridget. And all she could think of to say was a faint, "Sure."

BOB

How Far Would He Make It?

Bob's eyes fluttered open. Someone had shouted.
It might have been him.

His head hurt. With effort, he traced the memory back. Derrick had *hurt* him. *Derrick.*

Was his skull broken? With a groan, Bob pushed himself up on one elbow. He was in a bed in a room he didn't recognize. He stared in horror at the stains obscuring the pillowcase's tiny faded blue flowers. Blood. *His* blood.

Gritting his teeth, he touched his scalp. The wound was about an inch long, just above his temple. He pressed his fingers on his crew cut, tacky with blood. The skin had been split, but the skull underneath seemed intact.

A surge of relief rolled over him, followed immediately by a pulse of anxiety. What if he'd just exposed the wound to new germs? What if that half-formed scab was the only thing protecting him from a nasty infection right next to his brain? Back in the Middle Ages, you might not die from the battlefield wound, but from the infection that followed.

His stomach roiled as he thought of something else. He'd shouted as he woke. What if Derrick came back and hurt him again?

Bob strained his ears, but heard nothing. After pushing himself to a sitting position, he looked around. He was in a small bedroom, about twelve by fourteen feet. The walls were yellow pine, dotted with brown knotholes. The door was closed. The fir floor was bare.

Bob still couldn't believe what had happened. Derrick snarling at him to get in the trunk. The *Is that real?* gun that now seemed likely to be. The sickening crunch against his skull as he felt his bones turn to jelly. The engulfing darkness.

Bob was trembling, and it wasn't just from the chilly air. Things were horribly wrong.

When he swung his legs over the edge of the bed, there was a metallic clatter. Clamped around his ankles, over his socks, was what looked like a pair of handcuffs connected with a chain. A six-foot-long plastic-coated cable had been threaded through the cuff around his right ankle. The other end was looped around the leg of a desk a few feet away. The desk, made of aluminum and plastic, looked incongruously modern in the otherwise rustic setting. Under the desk was a built-in treadmill.

Bob was still wearing the same clothes in which he'd been taken. The same clothes he always wore. A plain black T-shirt and blue jeans. But what about his scarf? A second of panic before his fingers found it, still around his neck. No coat. His old white Nikes were nowhere in sight. Without the blanket's warmth, the cold was already sinking into his marrow.

In front of the treadmill desk, the single window was framed by white curtains. Outside, an expanse of white snow and massive evergreens.

Derrick had told Bob about this cabin, tucked away in the forest. No landline. No Wi-Fi. Just electricity and running water—if a storm didn't take them out.

Even if Bob managed to free himself, how far would he make it without shoes? He had researched frostbite, and it wasn't pretty. While he wasn't a big walker, without toes it would be even harder.

Between the bed and the treadmill desk was a nightstand overflowing with provisions. A brown Pyrex bowl filled with apples, bananas, oranges, pears. A bag of baby carrots. Six plastic water bottles. A loaf of Dave's Killer Bread. A brick of Tillamook cheddar. But no knife to cut it with. No utensils at all.

Nothing Bob could use to free himself. To attack someone. Or hurt himself.

The treadmill desk held, somewhat incongruously, a typewriter. A black Royal. Sitting next to it was a neat stack of blank white paper. The rest of the desktop was bare.

A single sheet of paper had been folded in half and propped on top of the typewriter. On it was scrawled,

Better start writing Eyes of the Forest. Or else!

Bob took stock. He was in an isolated cabin, injured, shackled. No one but his captors knew where he was.

Maybe hurting him had surprised Derrick as much as it had Bob. Or wouldn't he have put out painkillers, antiseptic, and bandages to go with the food? Other than the furniture, the room was bare. No TV, no magazines, no books. Not even any framed posters.

Nothing to distract him.

Bob shifted uncomfortably. Pressure, low in his belly. He had to pee. Presumably there was a bathroom someplace. He mentally measured the distance to the door and then the cable. It didn't seem good.

He got to his feet, briefly closing his eyes against a wave of dizziness. The cable pulled him up short before he reached the door. Bob leaned forward. The tips of his fingers just closed around the knob.

He pulled it open, revealing a narrow hallway and letting in air that was, if anything, even colder. From this vantage point, he couldn't see other rooms. It didn't matter anyway, because Bob couldn't reach them. Even if he managed to drag the treadmill behind him, it wouldn't fit through the doorway.

The pressure in his bladder was worse. "Derrick!" he yelled. "Derrick!"

No answer. The cabin was silent.

He was turning back when he spotted it. Squatting under the bed was a white ceramic pot the size of a mixing bowl. If it had been one-fifth the size, it might have been mistaken for serving ware. Perhaps a specialized vessel for cream or gravy that would appear only on Grandma's table at Thanksgiving.

But Bob knew exactly what it was. What it was for. A jordan, a jerry, a guzunder, a po, a chamber utensil, a thunder pot. A potty. A well-used item for centuries, across cultures, across continents, at least until the flush toilet had been invented.

"Oh, hell no," Bob said.

BRIDGET

Never Take Anything for Granted

Ajay followed Bridget down the hall to the cafeteria. "So why were you listening to that book in class?" With each step, the smell of old grease intensified.

"Because I love it." She grabbed a black plastic tray, then held up two fingers for the cafeteria lady. "Two tacos, please. With cheese." She turned back to Ajay. "Aren't you getting anything?"

"I bring my own lunch."

"Oh." In high school, that was true of hardly anyone. She associated bringing your lunch with people whose parents were too proud to take free lunch. Or people who were allergic to gluten or dairy or peanut butter. Or whose moms drew hearts on the outside of the paper bag and slipped a Post-it inside that said *Have a great day*.

The way her own mom used to.

"I've seen you listening to your phone in other classes." Ajay followed her to the big metal bowl of fruit. "I always thought it was music, but now I'm guessing it must have been a book. So what makes it worth getting your phone taken away?"

Inspecting an apple, Bridget tried to articulate her

feelings. "All the books in the Swords and Shadows series are amazing. They're filled with bravery, treachery, and sacrifice." She gestured at the fluorescent lights, the chipped linoleum floor, the hordes of students. "This is the boring real world, where Portland, Oregon, and Portland, Maine, are pretty much interchangeable. But in those books, there aren't any high schools or Walmarts or Taco Tuesdays."

"Hey, a lot of people like Taco Tuesdays," Ajay objected, following Bridget to the cashier.

"And in those books, you can never take anything for granted." She handed the cashier her cafeteria card. "You know how if you watch a movie, there's always certain characters you don't really have to worry about?"

"Like the cute five-year-old who keeps saying surprisingly wise things?" Ajay offered. "But no matter how bad things get, that kid always survives the vampires or the earthquake or the serial killer or whatever."

"Exactly." Bridget picked up her tray. "In the Swords and Shadows series, a five-year-old could and maybe would die. And the reader might even have to watch." She hesitated. Normally she sat on the edge of the cafeteria with a book and Ajay sat in the middle with friends.

"Want to eat outside?" he said. Now that the temperature was dropping, only a few people were sitting at the concrete benches and tables.

"Um, sure."

As they walked past his regular table, a couple of his friends nudged each other. He didn't seem to notice. In the far corner, Derrick was peering intently at his phone.

Outside, they found an empty table. Next to them, a couple was enthusiastically kissing. On the other side, a boy exhaled his vape smoke into his hoodie.

Ajay unzipped his backpack. "Okay, give me the basic rundown of the plot."

"For the whole series? That's like explaining how the entire world works to an alien who just landed here." But if anyone was up to the task, Bridget figured she was.

"Do the best you can."

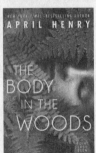